A WOLF BY THE EARS

After his parents died in a fire, Stephen Kirk expected to inherit a fortune, although his parents had left no will. But doubts are soon cast on his legitimacy. David Centre, a qualified solicitor, tries to unravel Kirk's complicated family history, only for his client to be arrested on a more serious charge. Stephen Kirk could remember nothing of his actions on the night his parents were killed. Centre soon discovers that a number of people had a keen interest in removing Harry Kirk. Suddenly there was no shortage of suspects.

A WOLF BY THE EARS

A WOLF BY
THE EARS

by

Roy Lewis

Dales Large Print Books
Long Preston, North Yorkshire,
BD23 4ND, England.

British Library Cataloguing in Publication Data.

Lewis, Roy
    A wolf by the ears.

    A catalogue record of this book is
    available from the British Library

    ISBN   978-1-84262-861-4 pbk

Dales Large Print is an imprint of Library Magna Books Ltd.

Printed and bound in Great Britain by
T.J. (International) Ltd., Cornwall, PL28 8RW

He who goes to law holds
a wolf by the ears.

–ROBERT BURTON,
Anatomy of Melancholy

CHAPTER I

Gordon Street was not situated in a slum area, for Linchester possessed none, but David Centre's was the only solicitor's office in Gordon Street and that in itself amounted to a condemnation of his practice. The local solicitors clustered, huddling together as though for protection, among the three narrow streets that faced the Town Hall and it was to this area that clients tended to gravitate. Nevertheless, the reception room and three office rooms in Gordon Street, above the bearded and retired naval captain who had decided that he ought to invest in an estate agent's business, was the only accommodation near the Town Hall that David Centre could get, setting up in practice for the first time in Linchester.

The trouble was in those first few months clients remained noticeable by their absence. It was for this reason alone that David Centre was particularly interested in the appointment made for him by his secretary, Janet Sanders. He had been lucky to get her: twenty-two, darkly attractive, splendidly efficient, she not only had previous experience of work in a solicitor's office but she had brown smiling eyes and a capacity for handling people that was more than useful in reception, while her telephone voice possessed a curiously husky warmth that would encourage at least the male clients to return.

'Stephen Kirk...' mused Centre, staring at his appointment book. 'Do you know anything about him?'

Janet nodded.

'I do, as a matter of fact. I knew him some years ago. He's about five or six years older than me but at one time, when I used to stay out with my aunt in Sandhill village, I used to play with Stephen Kirk. He was a nice lad, pleasant, but a bit posh we thought because he lived in the big house—'

'Big house?'

'Kirkley Hall. Just west of Sandhill village.'

'Are you trying to tell me that I might now have a *rich* client?'

'In Gordon Street, Mr Centre?' Janet laughed. 'I think I'd better disillusion you at once. Stephen Kirk left home a good seven years ago, as far as I can remember: he was sort of estranged from his parents.'

Centre frowned, staring at the name on the appointments book. Something about it rang a tiny bell in his memory. Solicitors could not advertise and could not tout for clients – their contacts had to be professional or social, and it often paid dividends to read the local papers with some assiduity, for the simple reason that when one met local dignitaries it was as well to know upon what their pomposity was founded.

'Kirk... Is this young man the son of Harry and Magda Kirk?'

'That's right. You'll have read about them recently, in the papers.'

As indeed he had. As he walked back into his office, leaving Janet sitting at the reception desk, he recalled reading about the fire at Kirkley Hall a few weeks earlier. It would seem to have started in the upper storey, in Harry Kirk's bedroom. Mrs Kirk had apparently run into the room to wake her husband but had herself been overcome by the smoke, and both had died in the fire. It had made headlines in the local press.

He sat down behind his desk, and eased his long legs. He placed both hands behind his head. One thing was for sure: whatever Stephen Kirk wanted, David Centre would be able to give the matter his virtually undivided attention, for there was hardly a flood of clients cascading through his doors. Centre sometimes wondered whether it was going to be worth it, leaving Canada, coming to England and starting out in a new career, a new profession. But then, it was necessary, if he was going to forget the past.

Kirkley Hall. Centre had driven past it once. He had taken the Aston Martin – the one real luxury in which he indulged on the ground that it was good for his image – and driven out west of Linchester towards Sandhill village. He remembered thinking how unspoiled the countryside was out there, although Sandhill itself was a little too prettily chocolate-box and twee for his tastes, with its tiny one-way bridge and its cottages nestling under a tree-garlanded hill. The developers hadn't stretched their predatory hands out towards Sandhill yet, and so Kirkley Hall itself also remained protected. He had seen it from the road, at the top of the hill, an eighteenth-century manor house, all solid stone grandeur, grey, somewhat forbidding, but possessing a splendid sweeping view down and across long meadows and a slow-moving trout stream to a faint haze of distant hills. The Kirks had lived in style.

And had died the same way.

The intercom buzzed, and Centre flicked the switch.

'Mr Kirk is here, Mr Centre.'

'Good, I'll come out to meet him, Janet.'

There was nothing like showing a client that he was wanted. Centre walked back to reception where Janet was talking to Stephen Kirk. He proved to be almost six feet in height, with a fine-boned face and a lock of hair which fell boyishly across his forehead. But it was his eyes that drew Centre's attention: they were a dark blue and held a trace of sadness. Not the sadness that would have

12

been occasioned by the loss of his parents recently, but something deeper, more permanent and in a way characteristic.

Centre put out his hand.

'Hello, Mr Kirk. I gather that you already know Miss Sanders.'

Stephen Kirk smiled; it emphasized the boyishness of his features.

'I do indeed. We're old friends. We used to know each other a long time ago, but I must say I wouldn't have recognized her as the scrawny kid I used to know!'

'I like that!' cried Janet in mock indignation. 'You weren't all that well fleshed yourself.'

'We all change, and in your case very noticeably. It's nice to see you again anyway, Janet.'

'It's a pity that it isn't at a more congenial time,' Centre said quietly. 'We heard about your parents, of course, Mr Kirk, and I'd like to express my condolences.'

Stephen's glance dropped and his face became pale.

'Yes... In a way, it's concerting that ... that I've come to see you.'

Centre nodded, then gestured towards the door.

'Yes, well, perhaps you'd like to come up to my office and we can talk there. Janet, I wonder whether you could rustle up a cup of coffee for Mr Kirk and one for me? This way, Mr Kirk.'

Centre led the way to the office and waved Kirk to the easy chair. With his own back to the window Centre could see his client's features clearly: it was an advantage, for the expression on a man's face could often belie the words that came from his lips.

'Now then, Mr Kirk, how can I help you?'

Stephen Kirk was obviously struggling to find the right words. With an impatient gesture he brushed the lock of dark hair from his eyes.

'I don't really know where to start.'

'The beginning?' suggested Centre with a smile.

'It's not as easy as that. I don't know where the beginning is, really. I'm all confused. Cousin John … do you know my cousin?'

'John…?'

'John Kirk. Of Kirk and Johnson. He's a solicitor too, over at Linthorpe. I thought you might know him. It was he who advised that I come to see you.'

Centre was none the wiser. He spread his hands wide.

'Well, what's the problem?'

Stephen Kirk hesitated momentarily, then plunged in with some decision.

'They say I'm illegitimate!'

There was a short silence. Centre observed the young man closely: he was even paler than before, and his eyes had gone blank.

'Who says this?' Centre asked.

'My cousin.'

'John Kirk?'

'No. Vasil Karnowski.'

'I'm afraid,' said Centre heavily, 'that you will have to be a little more explicit in your statements. I'm a bit lost.'

Stephen Kirk's hands were restless.

'You know that my ... my parents died recently, in a fire at Kirkley Hall. Well, a few days ago, Cousin John rang me to tell me that it would seem that neither my father nor my mother had left wills. It followed that on their intestacy I would be entitled to the estate. He then went on ... went on to tell me that I would have to take out letters of administration, but that when I did–'

'Yes?'

'The application would be opposed by Karnowski.'

Centre frowned and stared at the young man's pale face. He put his fingertips together in the approved judicial manner.

'Now let's get this straight, Mr Kirk. This Karnowski ... you said that he too was your cousin?'

Stephen nodded.

'I should explain. My father was not English. He was born in Poland but his parents took him to live in Germany. They also took with them two cousins – Johann and Vasil Karnowski. It was while they were living in Germany that my father met my mother – Magda Schneider.'

'Go on.'

'Well, after the war broke out they fled to England – my father, Harry, or Haren, as his name really was then – led them out. My mother Magda, and the two cousins, Johann and Vasil. Johann was in his teens then, Vasil was almost the same age as my father. When they got to England Vasil stayed on in London and more or less lost touch with the others. My father, my mother and my cousin Johann came down here and became British citizens. They took the name Kirk, Haren became Harry, Johann became John. Cousin John lived with the family while I was young, but after he qualified as a solicitor he moved to Linthorpe and set up practice there. He ... always remained close to my parents though.'

'I see. But Vasil Karnowski never changed his name?'

'No.'

Centre waited but Stephen Kirk said no more. He seemed lost in a reverie, staring out of the window. His eyes were vague fixed on nothing. At last, Centre said,

'And this Vasil Karnowski, it is he who claims you are not the legitimate son of Harry and Magda Kirk?'

Stephen's eyes flickered to his.

'Yes.'

He made no further comment and Centre was forced to draw him out further.

'Why did you not take this up with John Kirk?'

'How do you mean?'

Centre shrugged.

'Well, I would have thought that John Kirk was admirably qualified to deal with the matter for you. In the first instance he's a qualified solicitor, and secondly as a brother who is obviously involved he will have personal knowledge of matters that will be in issue. He's the obvious person to help you.'

Stephen looked at his hands.

'I did ask him,' he said reluctantly. 'He said that I ought to go to another solicitor. He said that he had advised Karnowski not to proceed with the matter, but that Karnowski was disregarding his advice. Cousin John said that he was disgusted about the whole thing, dragging Harry and Magda's names into court. He said that he wanted to wash his hands of the whole thing. Besides...'

He looked up to David Centre.

'...he said that he might get involved against his own inclinations, and it would hardly do to be acting for me.'

'I see what he means.'

Vasil Karnowski's motive for claiming that this young man was illegitimate was obvious. Centre had no idea what the Kirk estate would be worth, but if Stephen Kirk were declared illegitimate, the next of kin would take. They would be Vasil Karnowski and John Kirk. The solicitor obviously was quite sickened by Karnowski's threat of action and wanted no part in it, but he could not avoid involvement if the matter went to court. He would probably be called as a witness for Karnowski, and it would be difficult for him if he were acting for Stephen. No, it was certainly the right thing to do, to suggest that Stephen go to another solicitor.

And it was business for David Centre.

'What precisely do you want me to do, Mr Kirk?'

Stephen Kirk looked somewhat bewildered. He shrugged, and spread his hands wide.

'Well, ... advise me. I mean, what do I do now?'

Centre pondered.

'I think,' he said slowly, 'that in the first instance you must proceed as though nothing has happened. In fact nothing *has* happened yet, anyway.'

'But—'

Centre held up his hand.

'Your cousin was right in refusing to act for you and his sympathies obviously lie with you. I'll take the first opportunity of

18

going up to Linthorpe to see him and get the full story. But in the first instance we proceed as though Karnowski will be doing nothing.'

'But he's going to sue!'

'No, we don't know that he'll bring an action. He has threatened to do so. It might not come to that. You have not yet taken out letters of administration to the estate. We'll see what Karnowski does. He can either claim a grant himself, or he will allow you to take the grant and then contest your claim in court by asking for revocation of the letters of administration. So, the first thing we do is make application to the District Probate Registry for letters of administration. The fourteen days from the deaths are up so we can move at once.'

'And then?'

'Well, it depends. If Karnowski makes no move we'll proceed to administer the estate. As the only child of the deceased, you are entitled to the grant and the grant will enable you to deal with the property. It's then up to Karnowski to contest the grant.'

Stephen chewed his lip thoughtfully.

'Cousin John thinks he'll do it.'

'Cousin John may well be right – but Karnowski will have to show grounds. He will have to show that the grant was made to the wrong person – you – a person who is illegitimate but claiming to be a relative.'

Stephen flushed but said nothing for a moment. Centre read little in his expression, and when the silence lengthened he ventured:

'I must ask you, Mr Kirk: you have no reason to believe that you are *not* the legitimate son of Harry and Magda Kirk?'

Stephen flashed him a glance that was edged with anger.

'I have not! I was simply wondering, what the hell does Karnowski think he's playing at? What can he gain? How can he make out I'm illegitimate? I don't understand how he can think it, and I don't understand how he can behave in this way and drag their names into a court of law!'

Centre regarded his hands passively. He would have to choose his words with care; Stephen Kirk could boil over easily, and with some justification, for the matter was a delicate one.

'I'll speak to John Kirk first. He will be able to fill in some of the background, I've no doubt.'

'I've always been regarded, and have regarded myself, as their son.'

Centre nodded.

'That in itself is very important. But we must ask several questions. If Karnowski thinks you are illegitimate, this means there must be some doubt about your birth, or the fact of your parents' marriage.'

'You're suggesting that I was born out of wedlock. You're suggesting—'

'I'm suggesting nothing. I'm simply stating that Karnowski must have *reason* for claiming you are illegitimate. Now, can you produce the marriage certificate of Harry and Magda Kirk?'

'No.'

The answer was positive, so positive as to imply that Stephen Kirk had certainly made all the necessary checks for the whereabouts of the paper. There was no point in pursuing that line.

'Where were you born?'

'I don't know exactly. Somewhere on the Continent.'

'Birth certificate?'

'No.'

Centre grimaced. Stephen Kirk caught the movement and burst out,

'What difference does that make? My parents lived in this country since the early 1940s! They brought me up here – they called me their son! You're not trying to tell me that legally I would be regarded as illegitimate simply because I couldn't produce a piece of paper showing that a marriage was celebrated, or a birth recorded! Couldn't I claim … what do you call it … a common law marriage or something?'

Centre sighed.

'I'm not saying that the law regards you as

illegitimate. Indeed, it's up to Karnowski to prove that you're not. But let's just suppose that he produces some proof of some sort. We're in some difficulty then. You see, it's complicated by the fact that your parents weren't British at your birth, or living in this country.'

'How do you mean?'

'Well, the Legitimacy Act of 1959 states that even if parents never marry, a child will be deemed to be legitimate if at the time of the act of intercourse resulting in the birth both or either of the parties reasonably believed that the marriage was valid.'

'Doesn't that apply here?'

'It doesn't. It applies only if the father was domiciled in England at the time of the birth – and Harry Kirk was not. He had never lived in England, it would seem, and you were born before the family arrived here. The Act won't apply.'

Stephen was agitated. He rose to his feet and prowled around the room. He moved lithely, on the balls of his feet, but there was an anger in his movement.

'If they got married outside this country, what has English law to do with it anyway? What about Polish law, or German law?'

'English law is involved,' replied Centre patiently, 'because the estate is in England. The legitimacy question – well, I admit that if they were not married, according to our laws, that isn't the end of the matter. English law will regard you as legitimate if the law of your domicile of origin regards you as legitimate.'

'You've lost me.'

'Put simply, it's this way. If Harry and Magda didn't marry according to English law it's up to the country where your father was domiciled to decide whether you are legitimate or not.'

Stephen was aghast.

'You mean we'll have to go to Poland, or Germany?'

'No,' said Centre with a slow smile, 'the English court will take cognizance of the foreign law – it will act as though it were a court in a foreign country.'

'Hell's bells, it sounds crazy.'

'Perhaps it is, and you won't be the first to have said so, but that's the way it works. Roughly. In fact, it's a damn sight more complicated than that.'

Stephen Kirk was obviously distressed. His pacing had not stopped, and the frown on his forehead had deepened. Centre felt a real sympathy for the man. He stood up, came around the desk and put one hand on Stephen's shoulder. It was curious: Kirk was about twenty-eight, and David Centre was thirty-four – there was little difference in their ages and yet Centre felt very much the father figure.

'Don't worry too much about it. Look at the bright side. It may never happen – Karnowski may not challenge your grant of letters of administration. Secondly, even if he does, there's a lot on our side, and he'll have some difficulty in getting over it.'

'Such as?'

There was a gleam of hope in Stephen Kirk's eyes.

'Well, first of all, you weren't far wrong when you spoke of common law marriage. That doesn't apply here, but Harry and Magda did live together as man and wife for a long time – so there is a presumption that they were married, Karnowski will have to rebut, overturn, upset that burden to begin with. The burden of proof lies on him.'

'And secondly?'

'There's the presumption of legitimacy. If Karnowski claims that you are illegitimate it's again up to him to *prove* it – and the court will demand pretty cogent evidence.'

Stephen Kirk stared at him fixedly. His grin was a little twisted.

'It all depends upon whether he's got such proof, doesn't it?'

And if Karnowski didn't have, thought Centre to himself, as he said goodbye to Stephen Kirk, he would hardly threaten to bring an action.

Centre was unable to take the matter much further during the next few days. The application for letters of administration was duly made but Centre was unable to meet John Kirk. He rang the office of Kirk and Johnson in Linthorpe but was told that John Kirk would not be available for at least a week. He was in London and would not be returning until the following weekend. Centre decided the matter could wait.

Besides, he had other matters to attend to. Business suddenly began to pick up and there was also the question of getting a young legal executive to assist in the office. It was not one of the old managing clerks of yesteryear that he wanted, but a younger man who would be prepared to spread his horizons a bit, take the work as it came, and do some advising of clients. By the end of the week he had interviewed the right candidate – Charles Blake, short, twenty-six, fair thinning hair, intelligent eyes, and when asked to talk about himself, brief but relevant. Centre offered him more than he expected and the post was accepted with alacrity. It was a good sign.

The Stephen Kirk case did not remain far from his thoughts, nevertheless. It was not only that he was not hard pressed with work; the fact was, the case interested him. It was not the kind of problem that came the way of a solicitor in the provinces very often, and it was rather curious that it should have landed in his lap in this way – just when he was setting up in practice. It was certainly not the kind of problem he had expected to meet on coming to Linchester, which was after all just a town on the fringe of the commuter belt, with probably a few too many lawyers already living off the middle classes ensconced there, and little work of a business or industrial nature to elevate fees. It was true that there were a few light industries scattered just outside Linchester, and at Linthorpe: indeed, it would seem that Harry Kirk had built up a small fortune in two of the local factories. But the whole Kirk problem was a fascinating one, even if it never came to court: it raised points of international law that sent Centre diving back to his private international law books with delight.

But Kirk and private international law, this was one thing. Bread and butter was another. The opportunity to spread the butter a little more thickly came the following Monday. David Centre was instructed to defend a local resident, Donald Chambers, on a charge brought by the police under the Road Safety Act 1967.

There were many solicitors who regarded criminal litigation in the magistrates' courts as unproductive, ill-paid, and simply not worth the time and effort involved in preparing the case. As a young solicitor starting in practice, David Centre had other ideas. This case could be of importance for him and for his practice. Cases in the magistrates' courts were reported in the local press: it was the way a solicitor could get his name known. The thought was in his mind when he rose to his feet for cross-examination.

The police constable stood in the witness-box, solidly, a little pink-faced, with his eyes fixed on some point above the doors at the far end of the courtroom. The prosecuting solicitor had retaken his seat and was lolling back comfortably, one hand smoothing his bald head, the other hooked into his waistcoat. Don Chambers, dark-skinned, fair-haired, a bull-necked businessman in his late forties, looked up to Centre with shrewd eyes. Centre turned to address the policeman.

'I wonder whether you would mind just going over your evidence for me again, Constable Simmons.'

Constable Simmons had been schooled to answer direct questions only and kept his peace, his chin jutting forward. Centre applied himself to his notes.

'Now tell me, Constable, on the night in question, the twenty-third of April, I understand, you were proceeding down Allen Street on foot when you met Constable Stevens?'

'Yes, sir.'

'Would you like to go over again what you saw?'

Constable Simmons cleared his throat.

'Well, sir, I had just reached the spot where Constable Stevens was standing–'

'Which was–?'

'The corner of Allen Street and Grainger Road, sir. I had just reached him when we heard the squeal of brakes. We both looked up and across to the far end of the street and saw this car pulled up sharply against the kerb–'

'Outside Number twenty-three, Grainger Road?'

'Yes, sir, that's right.'

'Please continue.'

'I observed someone in the car attempting to get out. He was having some difficulty in doing so. I said to Constable Stevens that this looked a bit suspicious so he got back in the squad car with Constable Evans–'

'The car was parked at the street corner?'

'That's right sir, just where Constable Stevens was standing.'

Centre held up a hand.

'Before you go any further, may I ask – was the attention of Constables Stevens, Evans or yourself drawn to the car at the kerb *before* you heard the screech of brakes?'

Simmons shook his head.

'Can't say that it was, sir. It was the noise of brakes that drew our attention. It was as though he–'

'I don't really want your suppositions, Constable. You simply heard the brakes, and saw the car pulled in at the kerb.'

'And the man inside having difficulty getting out, sir,' added the policeman firmly. He was not a man to be prevented from having his say, if it was relevant to the police case. Centre nodded, and a slight smile pulled involuntarily at the corner of his mouth. He was aware of his client, Chambers, shifting uneasily in his seat.

'Right. Now then, as I understand the evidence that you have given, you suggested to Constable Stevens that he and his companion pull the squad car around towards the car now parked outside Number twenty-three, Grainger Road, and you–?'

'And I walked across the road to the car. To see what was going on.'

'What was going on?'

'Well, nothing.'

'I beg your pardon?'

'Well, sir, Mr Chambers had got out of the car by then and was just opening the gate to his house–'

'*Mr Centre.*'

Charles Miles, JP, leant forward, his heavy

head propped on a horny hand hardened by forty years in the farming business. As Chairman of the Bench, he was very conscious of his duties and punctiliously insisted upon due deference being granted his position; he also, in normal circumstances, was only too willing to accept long-winded arguments because he enjoyed his seat above the Clerk of the Court, where he was the cynosure of all eyes. But it was warm, it was near lunchtime, he was tired, and his keen little eyes were bored.

'Mr Centre, the morning is getting on and we have had all this already. I mean, do we have to go through the whole thing again?'

Centre smiled pleasantly enough.

'He has said it, sir, under the questioning of the prosecuting solicitor, but there are just a few points that I wish to be emphasized. If I may be indulged for just a few minutes longer...'

Miles creased his face in disdain and shrugged unhappily. Centre turned back to Constable Simmons.

'Mr Chambers was opening the gate to his house–?'

'And I stopped him.'

'At the gate of the house.'

'That is right. In the presence of Constable Stevens, who had got out of the car, I then told him that I suspected he was drunk and this he did not deny. I asked him if he would be prepared to come with us to the police station and he agreed. We took him in the squad car to Cannon Place Station and there he was given two breathalyser tests.'

'The result of the tests, according to the report, is that Mr Chambers was found to have more than the limit, of 80 milligrams of alcohol to 100 milligrams of blood, laid down in section 1(1) of the Road Safety Act of 1967.'

Centre paused and glanced at Chambers; the businessman's eyes were narrow. Centre addressed the policeman quietly.

'Are you familiar with the provisions of section 1 (1) of the Act?'

'Of course, sir, it's the section under which Mr Chambers was later charged.'

'Yes. What does the section say?'

'Well, sir, it states that it shall be an offence for anyone to drive or attempt to drive a motor vehicle when his blood alcohol count is higher than the prescribed limit.'

'Mr Chambers's proportion was greater.'

'More than twice as much, sir.'

'What else does the Act demand?'

Simmons peered at Centre in some surprise.

'I beg your pardon, sir?'

Centre smiled amiably.

'Does it not state that Mr Chambers should have been formally arrested before the breathalyser test was administered to him?'

'Well, yes, sir, but–'

'Did you formally arrest him?'

'Well, sir, I–'

'You *did* say that you *asked* him to accompany you to the police station.'

'Yes, sir.'

'He went voluntarily.'

'Yes, sir.'

'I see,' said Centre thoughtfully. 'Tell me, Constable, who lives at twenty-three, Grainger Road?'

The pink-faced young constable showed his surprise.

'Well, Mr Chambers, sir.'

'So I understand. I have only one more question, Constable. When you stopped Mr Chambers at the gate to his house – it *was* at the gate, wasn't it?'

'That's right, sir.'

'When you stopped him at the gate, did he have anything in his hand?'

Simmons looked further confused.

'I don't follow you, sir.'

'It's quite simple. What did he have in his hand?'

Simmons's brow cleared.

'Ah,' he said, 'yes, he did. He had the keys to the car he had just locked and left.'

There was a barely suppressed chuckle from the prosecuting solicitor. Centre looked briefly towards him – he could guess what the man was thinking. He would be saying to himself that David Centre was a foolish young puppy, that all the defending solicitor had now done was to re-emphasize in the mind of the magistrate the fact that Chambers had had more than the permitted alcohol count in his blood, and had the keys and was therefore in charge of the car. Centre smiled; the prosecuting solicitor had a shock coming. Centre turned to Charles Miles, JP.

'If the prosecuting solicitor does not intend to re-examine, your worship, I would like to submit that Mr Chambers has no case to answer!'

A chair scraped; the prosecuting solicitor. Charles Miles had woken up now, and his cunning little eyes were sharp, glancing from the Clerk to the Court to Centre, and back again.

'The grounds for your submission, Mr Centre?' he asked, in a firm voice. Centre raised his head.

'Section 1 (1) of the Road Safety Act 1967, the section under which Mr Chambers is being prosecuted, states that it is an offence to drive or attempt to drive a motor vehicle while unfit through drink or drugs. The defence admits that the breathalyser tests showed that Mr Chambers was in a condition where his blood/alcohol proportion was twice the permitted limit. But in the first instance, he was not formally arrested, as the

Act of 1967 demands, before the tests were administered. More seriously for the prosecution case, *he was not committing the offence in question when stopped by the police.*'

Charles Miles's heavy eyebrows came together.

'Explain, Mr Centre.'

David Centre smiled amicably.

'The Act states the offence, sir, as "driving or attempting to drive" the vehicle. Mr Chambers was doing neither. He *had* been driving the car; that is not disputed. But when spoken to by the police, and asked to go to the station for the breathalyser test, he was no longer driving or attempting to drive. He was entering his house. His journey, your worship, was over.'

He turned to look briefly at the prosecuting solicitor.

'My submission, therefore, is that there is no case to answer.'

And to the prosecuting solicitor's obvious chagrin Charles Miles rumbled from the Bench,

'And I'm inclined to agree.'

3

Charles Miles had left the courtroom and the prosecuting solicitor was in urgent consultation with a police sergeant outside the door as Don Chambers grinned expansively at David Centre, replacing papers in his briefcase.

'I have to offer you my thanks, Mr Centre. That was a smart demolition job you just did.'

Centre clipped the briefcase closed and looked up. His blue eyes were hard.

'No. You were fortunate, Mr Chambers, fortunate that you got out of that car when you did. Let's be frank about the whole thing. You got off the charge on a mere technicality, a playing with words. You didn't deserve to get off – but that's none of my business, of course. I just want to point out that you were lucky, very lucky. I wouldn't push your luck so hard again.'

'You charging me a fee for that piece of advice?'

Centre was unable to prevent the smile softening the grim line of his mouth. There was something – a directness perhaps – about Don Chambers that he liked, even though the man had behaved foolishly over the driving offence.

'No,' he replied, 'I'll make no charge for that. You're paying enough as it is.'

Chambers grinned; he had good teeth, white and evenly spaced, while his face was darkened and his fair hair bleached from the open-air existence that he obviously followed.

'Maybe so. Anyway, I'm glad that my pin struck lucky at least!'

'Pin?'

'Yep. Didn't choose you from the list in the phone book because of your fame. I haven't been long in Linchester and when this offence came up I had to get a solicitor, so, who was I to get, knowing nothing about any of them? So I got the Yellow Pages and I took a pin from my lapel, and – there you were!'

'I'm flattered,' said Centre in an amused tone.

'I gather you haven't lived very long in Linchester yourself.'

'That's right.' Centre moved away from the table and began to walk towards the doors at the far end of the courtroom, Chambers keeping pace just behind him. 'I took the office in Gordon Street just a few months ago.'

'How's business?'

Centre laughed, looking sideways at Chambers.

'Why? I thought you said you got value for your money today?'

Chambers shrugged broad shoulders.

'Well, I know how things can be when you come to a new town. Professional practice like yours, I mean, sometimes it's not easy to get things moving. Can't speak for a solicitor's practice, of course, but in the building and development line I known all about it. And about contracts, and late deliveries and all that jazz. First, it's tough to get started, and then it's hell to keep things buzzing.'

'Yes. I'm not unfamiliar with the building business myself.'

Chambers cocked an eyebrow.

'You say so? What d'ye mean? You practise with one of the building firms up country?'

'No. Not as a solicitor. Besides, it wasn't here, it was in Canada.'

They reached the doors and before Chambers could ask any more they caught sight of Constable Simmons, more pink-faced than ever, standing outside in the corridor with the police sergeant and a voluble prosecuting solicitor. As Chambers and Centre walked past, the prosecuting solicitor called after them. They stopped in the patch of sunshine thrown from the fluted windows just inside the main doors. The prosecuting solicitor glowered belligerently, his jowled face quivering.

'I'm advising the police to lodge an appeal, you realize that, Centre?'

David Centre smiled at the man's perspiring face and shrugged.

'I can't see on what grounds, but that's your business, and privilege.'

'I thought that I ought to tell you – we've got grounds, believe me. I just thought that you and your client should not be allowed to leave this court in a complete state of euphoria.'

'We are pleased,' Centre said with a mock gravity, 'that justice has been done, of course, but I would hardly have regarded our state as euphoric. However, perhaps we'll meet again.'

Centre and Chambers stepped out of the tall Victorian doors into the sunshine of the small tree-lined square that insulated the magistrates' courthouse from the main road slicing through the centre of Linchester. Centre confessed to feeling hungry but declined Chambers's offer of lunch, saying that he had to get back to the office.

'Pity. Er … that chap … will he lodge an appeal?'

'Possibly.'

'You don't seem worried.'

'I don't have to be. But seriously, Mr Chambers, don't get too anxious about it. It's over for now; let's just wait and see what happens.'

'Another conviction and bang goes my licence… Anyway, thank you again, Centre. Look, I'd like to call in to see you some time. Got some business I'd like to discuss with you.'

'Of what nature?'

'Well, I won't go into it now, but it's something I've been cooking up for some time. I'll get my secretary to ring yours some time during the next few weeks and we'll fix an appointment. Okay?'

'By all means, Mr Chambers.'

They shook hands and Chambers walked off. David Centre watched him go, walking with his head jutting forward belligerently, as though showing the world that he was a man with whom it could not trifle. Perhaps he was that kind of man. Centre made his way slowly back to the office.

Janet was sitting behind the desk in reception.

'Hello, Janet. Anything come in this morning?'

'Not really, Mr Centre. Two appointments made for next week.'

'Big deal.' Centre seated himself on the edge of the desk and grinned at the dark-haired girl facing him. 'You like the quiet life?'

'Gives me time to do my nails.'

'Some would never make such an admission. Be careful I don't sack you as redundant.'

'If you did, Mr Centre, who'd keep back the hordes of clamouring clients?'

'And if I did, who'd keep my appointments book tidy, and remind me of the time, and make my tea, not to mention coffee, and dust my desk, and mess up my papers–'

'I didn't–'

'No, you didn't, and you never have done, and don't you dare either. Anyway, I'd better get on.'

'What happened with Mr Chambers this morning?'

'He got off.'

'There you are! I always said it.'

Centre regarded her with a serious face, and nodded in slow deliberation.

'Always. I don't know what it was you always said, but you always did, and I wish I'd had the wit and intelligence to say it first. You're a lovely girl, Janet Sanders.'

And he meant it too, he thought to himself as he walked across the corridor to his office. Though perhaps he shouldn't have put it into words like that; it was hardly the way an employer should talk to an employee.

He took lunch in town at an indifferent restaurant and returned to the office by two-thirty. It was some time after three when Charles Blake, the legal executive, tapped on the door and entered at Centre's call.

'Message came in for you, Mr Centre. Or rather, two messages.'

'Yes.'

'First of all, it would seem that Mr Karnowski is going to do what you were telling me he had threatened to do. He has decided to contest the grant of letters of administration to Mr Stephen Kirk.'

'Has he now?' said David Centre thoughtfully. 'That's interesting. Look, Charles, this is likely to be a bit sticky – interesting case, but probably a bit involved. So I want you to do two things for me: first, I want you to get hold of a reputable enquiry agent. There was a firm I used when I was in articles in the Midlands – Carlsen's I think it was – see if they have any representatives in this area, and get hold of one of their men. We'll need him to do some ferreting around. The second thing is, I'll want you to try to get hold of Mr John Kirk of Kirk and Johnson. Now that Karnowski has decided to contest Stephen's claim to the estate it's essential that I get to see John Kirk at once.'

'Ah, well, Mr Centre, that's the second thing that I wanted to tell you anyway. The fact is, Mr John Kirk rang a few minutes ago, from London. He also has heard about the Karnowski suit and while he can't get down at once from London, he did say that you might find it convenient to lunch with him on Saturday at the Country Club.'

Centre raised his eyebrows.

'Next Saturday? Well, I'd hoped to see him earlier but I suppose that will have to do, in the circumstances. Good enough; confirm the arrangement, will you? Anything else?'

There wasn't, and Charles Blake withdrew. Centre settled back in his chair. There was one thing at least: he was going to be kept pretty busy during the next few weeks. He

41

had no illusions about the Karnowski case. It was not going to be easy: its complications could cause a great deal of difficulty. And it stood to reason that Karnowski must have some strong grounds for saying that Stephen was illegitimate.

Perhaps John Kirk would be able to provide the answers.

4

The annual dinner of the Linchester and District branch of the Law Society was held at Coram Hall, on the northern outskirts of Linchester. This was to some extent a sop to the country members: there had been complaints of recent years that the function was always held in Linchester itself, whereas the county possessed some admirable venues for a really splendid evening. The committee had taken the point at last, but had chosen Coram Hall because it amounted to a compromise – only seven miles from the centre of Linchester, but on a crossroads which linked up very well for most members in the county outside.

And it would seem that the choice was certainly proving successful. David Centre had no standards for comparison, of course, in that this was the first of the annual functions of the Linchester branch that he had attended, but the dining-room was certainly buzzing with conversation, the red and white wines were circulating freely, and every opportunity had been taken to exercise the wide choices available on the specially prepared menu. It was perfectly obvious that the management of Coram Hall had gone to some pains to ensure that the Hall would come into the committee's reckoning again next year: after all, a group of some one hundred and twenty people, who imbibed freely, and of such expensive wines, and who demanded an elaborate and wide-ranging menu, was not to be sneezed at.

Here, at dinner, Centre was sitting among strangers who made little or no attempt to draw him into conversation, although the man on his left had had the grace to suggest that they split a bottle of wine. No sooner had that been arranged, however, than the man had turned his dinner-jacketed back to Centre and plunged into conversation with his companions.

Centre thought sourly to himself that the meal was splendid but the company rather less so.

The speeches were standard for a Law Society dinner. Judge Everett spoke first, grinding on about the worthy Linchester Society, the long tradition of the legal profession, the degree of trust and even affection that it enjoyed in the minds of laymen everywhere.

'Bloody ostrich,' hiccupped the man on Centre's left.

The next speaker wore some chain of office. Centre looked at the menu and programme: Alderman James Lorey. A heavily built, florid man of middle height and grim, lined mouth that was now somewhat relaxed by the wine. When Lorey rose to his feet Centre saw the woman sitting next to him. She had long blonde hair, a smiling mouth, and bold, somewhat over-emphasized eyes. They were eyes that were never still; they flickered around the room as though seeking attention, demanding admiration and, thought Centre to himself, receiving it too, as he noted her glance pause and hold fixed points in the room from time to time. Some of the young men in their cups would no doubt be indulging in meaningful glances with her. She would obviously be with the alderman, but it didn't inhibit her. Lorey was speaking.

His speech was long and full of pomposity. Sycophantic laughter drifted around, but the woman at the alderman's side smiled her secretive smile in a way that made Centre feel that she would give the alderman trouble in more ways than one. Lorey was bumbling on about the work of the planning committee, holding it up as an example of democracy in action, and it seemed from the interest aroused among the audience that it was an issue of some local importance, though Centre, new to the area, knew nothing about it. But he caught the name of Sandhill Down several times.

He listened only vaguely; he watched the flickering eyes of the alderman's wife, guessed that she was at least fifteen years younger than the alderman, and noted Lorey's florid countenance and burly shoulders. The alderman carried little excess fat, and with his hair cut *en brosse* he exuded an impression of strength. A hard man, thought Centre, a dogmatic man – even a dangerous one. But, Centre suspected, a man who would be hard put to it to handle his wife. Her eyes said so, to the assembled gathering. Centre slouched in his seat with his brandy glass in his hand and, as the next speaker droned on, found himself drifting pleasantly into a doze.

Some miles away, there was a young man whose frame of mind was quite unlike Centre's. While Centre's attention drifted, and the solicitor dozed, the detective-sergeant was cold and disgruntled. While Centre felt satisfied after a good meal, the detective-sergeant was conscious of the fact that he had taken only a sandwich and a beer in the early evening. And while Centre stretched out in his chair, the policeman stood in the cold bare corridor of the upper storey of Kirkley Hall.

He'd no real official reason for being there, and this increased his unpleasant frame of mind. But he was a stubborn man, and disliked having a report sneered at. It was just what the Chief Inspector had done, sneered at his report on the fire at Kirkley Hall.

'Look, Sergeant,' he'd said. 'We've had a good whip-around there and there is simply nothing suspicious that we can go on. There was just the one seat of fire: the bedclothes. Mr Kirk must have been smoking in bed – we understand he took sleeping pills, he fell asleep, the bed caught fire, he was overcome very quickly by the smoke and flame. Shortly afterwards, after the fire started, Mrs Kirk came in and unwittingly, in opening the door, caused a tremendous down-draught. Her husband was still alive – but in trying to drag him out she was overcome herself. Now your report suggests that we bring in the lab boys. I can't agree. It's not necessary. There is no suspicion of foul play. Straightforward accident...'

And so the coroner had recorded at the inquest. Accidental deaths. But the young sergeant wasn't convinced. His lack of conviction had brought him back to Kirkley Hall tonight, when he could and should have been at home in front of a warm fire with his wife. He had no business here, and yet he couldn't leave it alone. Kirkley Hall drew him; yet he was annoyed with himself for there was nothing tangible to go on.

There was only instinct.

He paced through the burned-out corridor. It looked dangerous – though fortunately the fire brigade had quickly arrived and prevented the fire from spreading too far along the floor. He stood in the doorway of the bedroom in which the Kirks had died. The fire, starting in the bedclothes, had quickly demolished the ornate four-poster that had stood there in the centre of the room. The four-poster was now a few blackened sticks. The bodies, or what little was left of them, had been found half-way to the door. Mrs Kirk must have fought her way through the flames, dragged her husband from the bed and pulled him across the floor before being overcome herself.

The wall panelling, dry as tinder, had caused most of the trouble. The flames had seared right through the room, and the draught down the long, echoing corridor had caused the fire to spread quickly. It was amazing, really, the way the brigade had managed to prevent its spread.

He supposed the Chief Inspector was right. There was nothing to go on. Accidental death. And yet...

Slowly he walked down the charred stairs; flame-scorched they might be but they remained fairly sound. With his hands stuck disconsolately in his pockets he walked across the empty hall and let himself out. It was a cold, moonlit night. He closed the heavy oaken door behind him and ran his fingers over the iron studs hammered into the wood. The edge of one was sharp and something was caught against it – a small piece of cloth. Someone had torn clothing against it at some time.

The sergeant shrugged and walked away. To his left was the garage, now empty of cars. In front of the house was a small shrubbery, extending down towards the garage. As he walked past it something glinted in the moonlight.

The sergeant took out a torch and flicked its switch. The metal object in the shrubbery turned out to be a small hip flask. He stretched out his hand to pick it up and stopped; he had the impression that the flask had not been dropped or thrown down – rather, from its location, it would seem to have been deliberately thrust under the bush. As though for concealment.

The beam of the torch wavered over the side of the flask. Then it was still. Thoughtfully, the sergeant broke off the stem of a four-foot Michaelmas Daisy and inserted it through the neck of the flask, then eased the container out from under the bushes with considerable care. He sniffed at it.

It still proved nothing. It still meant nothing. But it was interesting. The flask that he had found under the bushes had been used to carry a small quantity of paraffin.

5

On the Saturday morning David Centre drove out to the Linchester Country Club. He was early for his appointment with John Kirk so he walked around to the tennis courts at the back of the club. For a while he stood watching the players in action. He had played quite a bit himself in Canada, but he couldn't recall having had a game at all since his return to England. He went into the bar and ordered a drink. No question as to his membership was raised and he sat in the corner of the half-empty room and stared out of the window across the golf course. It was a sunny morning, but a light breeze lifted the red and white flags and made them dip and dance.

Things were beginning to sort themselves out, at least. This afternoon he should be able to get some information from John Kirk about the whole matter of Stephen's illegitimacy and this he would be able to transmit – what was relevant, at least – to the enquiry agent whom he had engaged. Centre's mind slipped back to the interview he had conducted that morning. He had asked Charles Blake to get hold of a man from a reputable agency and Blake had fixed an appointment for eleven that Saturday.

The enquiry agent's name was Paul Iles.

Centre had met him with considerable interest. During the course of business a solicitor had occasion to use enquiry agents for a large number of matters – the discovery of spouses who had run off, or who were failing to pay maintenance, the serving of writs, the obtaining of information to support the case that the solicitor might be conducting. During his period of articles in the Midlands, and since, David Centre had met a number of these people and in his experience they fell into a general pattern. They were more often than not ex-policemen. Sometimes retired, sometimes not; occasionally he had come across men who had left the Army and the Military Police, and there had in fact been one ex-major he had dealt with, but that particular man had not lasted long. However, in Centre's experience these men were invariably on the wrong side of forty and considerably so, heavy in build, careful, nondescriptly dressed and if not seedy, well, a little *depressed*. Paul Iles in no way fitted that description. He was a little above middle height and his brown hair was cut fairly short; he had smiling, dark eyes, and a face that looked as though it would suit a second row forward on a rugby field, with his broken nose and scarred forehead. He had good teeth, which his smile showed to advantage, and his suit was dark and well cut – though of a material that could be described as serviceable rather than expensive. Nevertheless, the overriding impression that he gave was one of a certain athletic elegance: he would, Centre had decided, be a useful man to have on one's side in a rough-house.

'Good-morning, Mr Iles. Do sit down. You're from the Carlsen agency, I gather.'

'That's right, Mr Centre. I'm what you might call their man in Linchester – for the time being, at least.'

'Ah yes, well, I made use of the Carlsen agency when I was working in the Midlands and they seemed to produce good results–'

'Our sales patter will tell you that we *always* do, Mr Centre,' Iles said, grinning. Centre returned the grin.

'For the prices and fees charged they'd have to do that.'

'You get what you pay for, Mr Centre. The higher, the better: not always an accurate assessment of quality, but with us I think it is.'

'Good enough. Well, we might as well get down to brass tacks straight away. The assignment isn't an easy one – not a good one to start our acquaintance with.'

'That depends upon how quickly we get what you want.'

Not *if*, but how quickly, Centre noted. There was a certain breeziness about Paul Iles that reminded him of many young men that he had known in Canada: it was a quality that came of self-confidence, and a self-confidence bred upon ability and results.

'We'll see. I'd better fill you in on the facts as far as I know them first of all – and you will treat all I say as confidential, of course.'

'It's in our brochure, Mr Centre, and engraven on our hearts.'

Centre smiled and continued.

'The matter concerns the legitimacy of my client. I said it is a difficult one because his parents were not British citizens when they married, if they married at all. The few details we have here are on this sheet – you will have to chase them up. It's likely to mean some ferreting around in Germany, and perhaps Austria. The problems are obvious.'

Iles frowned, and his face took on an even more battered appearance.

'Hmm... We've got an agency representative in Berlin. Austria, I'm not so sure. In a civil case like this I think we have some contacts that we can use, but it might mean in the long run that I'll have to go over personally. I'll sort that out anyway. What is it precisely that you want?'

Centre fished in the drawer and extracted the buff folder containing the papers that he had received from Stenson, the barrister from whom he had received an opinion.

'I've taken advice on evidence from counsel, to work out just what we need. The best thing I can do is to outline to you what our problem is, and then you'll see just what we want.'

'Sounds fine.'

'Good. Now then ... my client, it is claimed, is illegitimate. It's up to the other side to *prove* this, but if we assume that a *prima facie* case is made out, how do we rebut it? Of course, if we could produce a birth certificate naming the parents this would in itself raise the presumption of legitimacy – but we can't, at present. My client was born somewhere in Europe, probably Austria; we don't even know if the birth was registered. So where does that leave us?'

He paused; Iles was listening closely.

'Since marriage is obviously relevant to the issue our proving it will go a long way towards establishing our case. There are several ways we can prove a valid marriage: we can prove it from cohabitation and re-pute, that is, the fact that they lived together as man and wife–'

'Which I presume they did.'

Centre nodded.

'But I suspect,' he added, 'that the other side will claim this isn't enough, and will undermine the presumption by producing

53

verbal evidence as to pedigree or something
… you know, statements made perhaps by
the father that our client was not his
legitimate son and so on.'

'I see.'

'Those are matters I'll be checking on.
Anyway, secondly, we can prove the marriage
by producing someone who was present at
the wedding. This is difficult; the only people
we know who were positively with the couple
at the relevant time, and who could have
gone to the ceremony if there was one, are on
the other side – and they'll deny there was a
ceremony, it seems. But if you can dig up – I
don't mean that literally – someone who was
present, then we can get an affidavit from
him and you'll be my friend for life.'

'You can tell me the likely places where
this marriage might have taken place?'

'Not just at the moment. I shall be meeting
Mr John Kirk this afternoon, and I hope to
establish such facts from him. I have made a
rough outline of the probable journey they
took, based on my client's recollections from
conversations with his parents some years
ago. It's all here in this folder.'

'Fine.'

'Now we'll also have to prove that not only
did the marriage take place, but that it was
a formally valid marriage.'

'You mean that there's a difference?'

'The marriage ceremony,' explained

54

Centre, 'might not have complied with the formal requirements of the country in question. This will have to be my problem, however. If you can discover proof of the celebration of the marriage, then I'll take the necessary steps to get an expert witness to state that the certificate constitutes a formally valid marriage proof. And, of course, if we can do that, we're more or less home and dry, for if the parents *were* married then my client will be presumed legitimate and it takes very cogent evidence to show that he was in fact not the child of the marriage: the courts don't like bastardizing the issue of a marriage.'

Paul Iles stood up; he was a businesslike young man.

'Fine. Let me have the papers, then. You'll want me to try to turn up first, a birth certificate, or second, the fact of a marriage ceremony and its place; third, a certificate proving the marriage, or otherwise some character who will swear that he was present at the ceremony.'

'Possibly one of the witnesses, or the priest.'

'Anything else?'

'No, not at this stage. But I'd like you to keep in touch and let me know how things are developing.'

'Surely. I'll get started right away, Mr Centre. As soon as I turn anything up I'll let you know. Er … just one thing…'

Centre raised an eyebrow.

'Cost,' explained Iles. 'Telephone calls and trips to Europe are expensive. I imagine that your client will want to fix a ceiling?'

'My client has told me that no expense is to be spared, if it is necessary. I think you will appreciate that there is a considerable amount of money involved, but that the question of money alone is not uppermost in my client's mind.'

'I understand.'

Centre thought that Iles probably did understand – understood that for Stephen Kirk there was more than the money to think about, there was the stain of illegitimacy to be wiped from his own brow, and there were the imputations that were now necessarily being levelled against his parents. Both of these were emotional issues divorced from the money – though that in itself was a strong enough motive. Paul Iles couldn't know just how large the estate was. There was not only the matter of Harry Kirk's estate, there were also the shares and stock that over the years had been handed over to Magda. Kirk had obviously felt it safer to transfer a considerable amount into her name just in case the bankruptcy courts beckoned at any time. And now there it all was, not yet fully valued, but at Centre's guess somewhere in the region of one hundred thousand pounds.

And Harry Kirk had made that from

virtually nothing…

'Mr David Centre?'

The solicitor looked up from his view of the Country Club golf course to see a man advancing towards him past the bar. The speaker was tall, slim and elegantly dressed. He was in his middle fifties, perhaps leaning towards sixty, but where many of his contemporaries would have spread at the waist, this man bore a youthful appearance physically, and his suit was of a modern cut, his tailors immaculate in their taste. At Centre's nod he smiled, and extended his hand. He had a broad face, but a handsome one, with flaring eyebrows and narrow, piercing eyes. His hair was straight, grey, and parted with precision. He had, decided Centre, style.

'Yes, I'm David Centre.'

'Perhaps you will permit me to buy you a drink.'

Centre smiled, considering.

'Well, I don't know why you should, but I'll have no objection if you do.'

'The reason is simple. You are kind enough to act for my nephew. My name is John Kirk. Whisky?'

John Kirk's accent was impeccable, but in a sense too impeccable – it was obviously the result of careful control. He could have known little English when he came in from Poland or wherever it was – but he, and Centre supposed his cousin too – had obviously taken great pains to assimilate customs, tones, accents and behaviour. They would obviously have wanted to fit in. And it would seem that they must have done: Janet had mentioned that she understood that John Kirk had had Harry Kirk's facility for making money. Perhaps it was a family trait.

Kirk returned with the drinks.

'Your good health, Mr Centre.'

But it was there, nevertheless, now that Centre looked for it. A slight intonation, a clipped Central European phrasing.

'And yours, Mr Kirk. I'm glad I've met you. I was hoping we would be able to speak together soon.'

Kirk waved his glass in deprecation.

'Yes. I must apologize, but I have been so tied up these last two weeks in London. As a solicitor yourself, you know how difficult it is to find time to do anything when a High Court judgment is in the offing. However, as soon as I heard that Karnowski was proceeding with his suit I decided that I would have to get in touch with you as soon as possible, to render what assistance I could.'

'I'm sure that you'll be able to help considerably, Mr Kirk – particularly over the question as to what precisely happened when you and your cousin came to England.'

Kirk stared at Centre for a moment, frowning slightly. Then he half turned towards the door.

'Yes … I think, Mr Centre, that we might take our drinks through here. Since our conversation is to be somewhat of a … er … confidential nature, I have taken the liberty of engaging a private room here at the club, where we can lunch quietly without being disturbed. May I lead the way?'

'Of course.'

They walked through the lounge and down the soft-carpeted corridor to a dark oak door, where a white-jacketed waiter stood as though on sentry duty. He leaned forward at their approach.

'Mr Kirk?'

His tone carried the deference that servants showed towards club members of quality, and, supposed Centre, wealth.

'This way, sir.'

It was a small room, with a magnificent view across the golf course, curving upwards to a belt of trees on the ridge a half mile away.

'A pleasant setting, is it not? You must join the club, Mr Centre. I will propose your membership.'

Centre murmured non-committally and they sat down with their drinks. John Kirk stared at him quite openly, as though searching for his character in his face. Kirk's eyes were grey and held, thought Centre briefly, a hint of sadness. The thought reminded him of recent events.

'I think,' he said, 'I should first express my condolences.'

The grey eyes slipped away, and Kirk was looking out towards the distant ridge. He was silent for a moment, and then he looked back to Centre.

'You are kind. It was a great shock. We were cousins only, Haren and I, but we were close in our relationships. And Magda too... Indeed, it is one of the reasons why I am so thankful to you, for taking the case of Stephen's. I am fully aware that it will not be an easy one.'

You'll know more about its difficulty than I, Mr Kirk.'

The grey eyes regarded him soberly.

'Yes. But you will realize that it was a considerable shock, hearing that my brother Vasil intended to bring this action. A shock, and a great pain, on top of the loss that I had sustained...'

'I quite understand.'

There was a knock at the door and the waiter came in with the menus. Silence fell for a few minutes while they studied the choices available, then they placed their orders and the waiter withdrew.

John Kirk looked down at his whisky glass.

'I hadn't seen my brother Vasil for some years, you know, until he suddenly appeared after the funeral service. It was then that he approached me and asked me about the legal position. You know, he did not give a single damn about what had happened to Haren and Magda. Not a single damn about the way that they died…'

His face seemed suddenly drawn, and he looked older.

'But then, he hadn't maintained contact with them the way I had. Even so, he was so cold … so indifferent to the manner of their deaths. So indifferent to my loss, and to Stephen's feelings too, for that matter. It was as though Haren and Magda had not existed for him as people. It was as though they were … what is the word … ciphers only. Cardboard figures that, once removed, would lead him to the kind of riches he had always desired and never achieved.' His eyes were clouded. 'He cared nothing for the way they died. It was terrible, that they should have died together like that. I miss them, I miss them both. You might think it strange, Mr Centre, but in a way I miss Magda even more than Haren, my blood cousin. But for so long she was, well, a mother and indeed more than a mother to me. I was only pleased that of recent years I was able to repay some of her kindness…'

He broke off, and smiled sadly in some embarrassment.

'I should explain that I lived with Haren and Magda until I qualified, and then after I went to Linthorpe I handled all Magda's affairs. In this way I was able to be of assistance to her in these later years. She was a fine woman.'

He toyed with his whisky glass, holding it gently in his slim fingers.

'It is curious, nevertheless, how you can never do enough for anyone. Magda was like that. I was always in her debt, do you know? Even at the end I remain in her debt, for the pleasure that she gave me, the kindness that she showed me, the warmth and the affection and the strength – I was never able to repay it.'

He smiled wistfully.

'And yet, I *could* have repaid her in a sense, that last afternoon of her life. Do you know, Mr Centre, she need never have died in that holocaust? You see, I was at Kirkley Hall on the afternoon of the fire, speaking with Haren... Magda was there and asked me if I would give her a lift to Grangetown. Normally I would have been only too pleased to take her – she intended staying there overnight – but I had an appointment at six, in Southcliff, all of sixty miles away. So I had to refuse her, and I telephoned for a taxi for her and then I drove to Southcliff.'

He paused.

'It would seem that after I left she cancelled her taxi, cancelled her trip to Grangetown. If she had gone, if I had taken her, she would have been safe, she would not have died with Haren. They shook me awake, at my hotel in Southcliff, to tell me about the fire. I hadn't intended staying at Southcliff, you understand, but my car broke down so I had no choice. When they told me about the fire my first thought was that Magda, at least, would be safe. But she wasn't – she had been caught in that fire.'

His voice trailed away and he shrugged.

'It's all over now.'

'You can't blame yourself.'

Centre made no attempt to keep the sympathy out of his tone: John Kirk had obviously felt the loss of his cousin and his cousin's wife keenly.

'That's easily said... And now there's Stephen.'

John Kirk seemed lost in thought. The waiter entered again and placed their orders before them. Kirk was silent, eating, and Centre was too inhibited by the man's air of gloomy reflection to strike up conversation, and bring it around to the main subject on issue – the Karnowski action. He was somewhat surprised, nevertheless, when Kirk suddenly said,

'We never found their wills.'

Surprised though he was, Centre quickly realized that the whole topic of the death of his cousin must have been preying heavily upon Kirk's mind. The man was obviously struggling to maintain a normal conversation and yet continually his mind was sheering back to the events that had so shattered him recently, even to the exclusion of discussion of the Karnowski case.

'Neither Haren's will, nor Magda's. I knew what they contained, but that's not good enough. In fact, Haren left a small legacy to me, but the estate to Magda – though if she predeceased him I was to be the beneficiary. He'd cut out Stephen... Magda's will – again I was a beneficiary, but she left the bulk of her estate to Stephen. But both wills were missing. It would seem that both must have been destroyed in the fire, and there were no copies kept in my office. Haren had insisted that it wasn't necessary. But of course, though Haren would have left the estate to me rather than Stephen it's really only justice, the way things turned out – justice that Stephen should inherit. Upon the intestacy, I mean. After all, I have no need of Haren's money.'

His brow darkened.

'At least, Stephen would have got the justice due to him if Vasil had not–'

The waiter tapped, and entered the room nervously.

'Excuse me, gentlemen, but I have a message for Mr John Kirk.'

'You're speaking to him.'

The waiter gestured towards the lounge.

'There's a telephone call for you, sir. If you

come through the lounge you can take it in the manager's office.'

Kirk's flaring eyebrows were raised in surprise.

'A telephone call for me? Here?'

The waiter nodded positively.

'He said it was important, sir. A Mr Martin.'

Centre heard Kirk suck in his breath. When he glanced at the older man he seemed to have paled. Kirk was silent for a moment and then, after a quick flicked glance in Centre's direction, he muttered an apology and hurried down the stairs. He seemed agitated.

Centre watched him leave, and after a moment returned to his meal. It was pointless waiting – there was no telling how long Kirk would be. While he ate he thought about what Kirk had said. Strange that Harry and Magda Kirk had left no wills; indeed, strange that they had kept no copies in John Kirk's office. John Kirk could, of course, have sworn to the contents of those wills but it would not have been like the man: he obviously felt that it was only right that Stephen should inherit. And in a way, perhaps, it was justice that Stephen should take the property rather than John Kirk, who had said that he had no need of it anyway.

But life could play strange tricks. As it was playing a trick on Stephen Kirk now, with the advent of Vasil Karnowski's action.

It was only a few minutes before Kirk returned, and sat down at the table. The older solicitor's face seemed drawn but some of his colour had returned.

'I'm sorry about that, Centre. A matter of business... And I must offer apologies too for the way I've been prattling on about Haren and Magda – though in a way you might find it helpful to know what sort of person Magda was. What you are really concerned with, of course, is the Karnowski action.'

Centre nodded.

'I'd appreciate any light you can throw on the matter, Mr Kirk.'

'Yes. Well, I'll do what I can. I think that what I must do is to put the whole thing into perspective for you. Explain what happened, all those years ago... You see, we were Polish in origin. Haren's parents took me to Germany – Haren, and Vasil and me, for our parents were dead. Haren's father opened a delicatessen but it was the thirties, and, you must understand, we were of Jewish extraction. They ... they murdered Haren's father and mother in 1938.'

He was silent for a moment, then pulled himself together with an effort.

'Haren told us, Vasil and me, that he was taking us back to Poland and he had decided to take with him his girl, Magda. We started in 1939 but the movement of events caught us in Austria, and it was then that we decided, or Haren did, to head for England. We were smuggled out by patriots and it cost us all we had – things were further complicated by the fact that, just before we left, Stephen was born of Magda.'

Centre opened his mouth to speak – John Kirk had omitted something. Then he thought better of speech as he realized the significance of the omission.

'We came to London–'

'Mr Kirk,' interrupted Centre. 'Before you go further, can you give me the itinerary of your journey from Germany? The towns you visited–'

Kirk was smiling faintly and reaching inside his jacket. He pulled out a foolscap envelope and passed it across to Centre.

'I realized you would want such information. You will want to check at synagogues for a possible marriage, and at registries for a birth certificate. For what it is worth, the route is detailed here.'

Centre didn't like the implication; it boded ill for his client's case.

'We came to London,' continued John Kirk, 'and my brother Vasil stayed on there, and took a job as a shipping clerk. He still does the same job. Haren wanted better things and eventually came to start business in Grangetown. He prospered. I was younger than Vasil and I – I opted to go with Haren. I was closer to him than to my brother. I lived with Haren and Magda – Haren paid for me to complete my education and helped me to obtain articled service. When I qualified I left Kirkley Hall, which Haren had just bought and went to Linthorpe, into partnership with Johnson. He died in 1952; I am now the only principal. I never went back to live with Haren … perhaps I should have done, for then Haren and Stephen … they might not have quarrelled. No matter. But Haren was hurt … he threw his son out because he was angry that Stephen could have done that thing to him. But I must not bore you with family squabbles – other than the one which now concerns you.'

He squared his shoulders.

'The fact is that as soon as Vasil Karnowski heard that Haren and Magda had died he came to see me. The first time in twenty years. I was forced to tell him that they had died intestate. It was then that he told me what he intended doing. I shouted at him; I pleaded with him. But,' he added bitterly, 'it would seem that I have no control over my brother.'

His grey eyes flickered to Centre, listening silently.

'I was furious. I told Vasil that I would have nothing to do with it. He pointed out that I too would benefit but when I told him that I

68

had no need of Haren's money he simply said that *he* had – and that he intended going through with this thing. He was going to drag it out, drag Magda's name through the courts, smirch her and Haren too. It sickened me ... particular since I realized I could not stop him, and I could do little to help the son of Haren and Magda. So I washed my hands of the whole affair, and knowing that I might be called by Karnowski as a witness, I told Stephen to come to you.'

Centre found himself unable to resist the question.

'Why me, Mr Kirk?'

John Kirk was frank.

'A young man starting in practice usually has time on his hands. Time he would be pleased to devote to a case such as Stephen Kirk's. I had every confidence that you would pursue the matter with energy.'

Centre pursed his lips thoughtfully. The question had to be asked.

'You could not dissuade Karnowski from his action,' he said quietly. 'That must only mean that he has grounds for believing Stephen to be the natural, and not the legitimate, son of Haren and Magda Kirk.'

John Kirk looked tired.

'To the best of my belief,' he said, in a voice tinged with sadness, 'Haren and Magda never went through a ceremony of marriage.'

CHAPTER II

Mr Justice McIver sat stiffly in his chair. It was a matter of pride with him that no matter how long the hearing might be, and everyone admitted that in Chancery a hearing could be inordinately long, his bearing did not change. He remained stiff-backed, alert, and in command of the situation. It was, of course, a legacy of his background. He had started the last War in the Inns of Court Regiment, he'd commanded a mule battalion in Sicily: there had been the staff course in 1944 and then the Legal Division of the Control Commission for Germany.

The Ministry of Justice for the British Zone in Hamburg, the Court of Appeal for the British Zone in Cologne ... those had been the days. The Chancery Bench rarely produced such challenges, though it was possible that this case, with its overtones of Austrian, German and English law looked promising. He had been appointed to the Chancery Bench in 1963, after coming back to his practice at the Bar for a few distinguished years. And on this Bench he retained his military bearing, his eagle eye, his swift logical summing up of a situation and his appreciation of courtroom tactics and strategy. He was nobody's fool. He was a member of a distinguished profession, composed of men of power and independence, curbing by their wisdom the excesses perpetrated by an ignorant Parliament and an over-zealous Civil Service, and if this case before him now tended to emphasize issues that were personal rather than far-flung and policy-making, well, no matter, he would yet act with justice in all events.

He looked over his glasses and counsel rose to face him. Warrender spoke first: McIver knew him quite well, an Inner Temple man, Oxford and the Army before he joined Lincoln's Inn and took up a Chancery practice.

'I represent the plaintiff, my lord.'

'And I speak for the defendant, my lord.'

Stenson, junior counsel, making a bit of a reputation for himself in Chancery. Could be an interesting case, this. McIver's eyes flickered down the courtroom to the solicitors: the man acting for the prosecution of the plaintiff's case was familiar. Lockwood, that was his name, prominent City firm specializing in Chancery matters. The defending solicitor, he'd be the country man, unknown to McIver. Presentable young chap ... good straight back.

'I would,' said McIver, 'first of all commend the assiduity with which both parties have

71

prepared their cases. I have been much impressed with the quality of the affidavits presented. They do indeed make my task much easier. Many of the issues seem already resolved, but may I ask whether you wish to cross-examine witnesses upon any of these affidavits?'

Stenson looked across to Warrender and then said,

'That is certainly my intention, my lord.'

'Then you will have seen to it that the relevant parties are in attendance.'

'They are in attendance, my lord,' replied Warrender, jerking nervously at his robes.

McIver nodded, pulled his pad closer to him and settled back in his seat.

'Then perhaps we can proceed, Mr Warrender.'

'Certainly, my lord. The first person to be examined will be Mr John Kirk, formerly Johann Karnowski.'

David Centre turned his head to watch John Kirk come forward. Kirk showed no sign of emotion, but neither did he even so much as glance at his brother, Vasil Karnowski, as he passed him. He was obviously hating the whole thing and his answers to Warrender as he was taken through the main body of his affidavit were short and concise.

As Kirk gave evidence Centre found himself looking again at Vasil Karnowski. He was completely unlike his brother. Janet had told Centre that Harry and John Kirk were alike not only in their business instincts and ability but also in their physical appearance. Vasil Karnowski was utterly different. He was tall, with hunched shoulders, bald head, and predatory nose. His face was pinched and his eyes hard. Centre had met him during the first hearing before the Master in Chancery when the case had been fixed for the witness list and had been impressed by Karnowski's unprepossessing appearance then. He had had no reason to change his views since: Vasil Karnowski was a man whom it would be difficult to like. Indeed, if he had any good points, he seemed singularly adept at disguising them. It was strange that two cousins – Harry and John – should look alike, but that the two brothers should not.

Karnowski's wife sat beside him. She was English, of well-built peasant stock, it would seem. Her features were stolid and unemotional, though in his interview with Centre, John Kirk had hinted that he suspected Elaine Karnowski exercised considerable influence over Vasil and indeed was perhaps pushing him hard in this suit.

Warrender was handing the witness over to Stenson, and Centre directed his attention towards John Kirk. The handsome face seemed in repose, but his answers were less guarded in tone: it was as though he wanted to help Stephen's case as much as he could. Unfortunately, as Centre well knew, the only information that he could give was negative to Stephen's chances of success.

'You stated that you left Germany in 1938?'

'That is right. Our parents had been killed by the Nazis and we left, intending to return to Poland. We were forced to enter Austria and we quickly found ourselves in trouble there.'

'When you say "we", you mean yourself, your brother, your Cousin Haren and his wife.'

Kirk hesitated; it was the word 'wife', Centre realized. Then he nodded. Stenson seized upon it.

'Is it not true that shortly before leaving Austria, your cousin married Magda?'

'I am sorry, but there was no marriage, either before we left Germany or Austria. There was no time in Germany; we were anxious to leave and Magda's parents had begged us to take her with us. In fact, at that time, I do not believe that it was in Magda's mind to marry my cousin.'

'How long did you stay in Austria?'

'We managed to get out, via an underground organization, in late 1940. It was then that we came to England. So we were in Austria for about a year.'

'During which time the son, Stephen, was born?'

'He was a baby when we left Austria for England.'

'At what time was the attachment formed between your cousin and Magda?'

'Early in 1937 ... no, it would be in 1938, shortly before we decided to leave Germany.'

'And it was then that they got married?'

'I am sorry. As far as I am aware there was no marriage.'

'You remained together, as a family, during the whole period of time in Austria?'

'During the whole period.'

'There was no time when you were apart? No few weeks, no odd days?'

'We were not apart for any length of time.'

'When you say length of time you prevaricate, Mr Kirk. What I am asking is this. Is it not possible that the two ... ah ... lovers could have taken a few days away from you and Vasil Karnowski? Is it not possible that they could have got married during that period?'

Kirk nodded vigorously.

'Ah, yes, it is possible. All that I am saying, in truthfulness, is that I do not know of any ceremony of marriage. I am not saying and have never said that they did *not* get married. There would obviously have been times during that year when they could have got away to the synagogue to marry but I simply say they did not do so to my knowledge.'

'One moment.'

Mr Justice McIver leaned forward, peering over his glasses at Kirk's upright figure.

'I must confess to a little puzzlement,' the judge remarked. 'You say that they *could* have got away to marry, but that if they did, they never told you. Explain to me, Mr Kirk, is there any reason why they should *not* tell you, if they had got married? Particularly so, if in fact a child was on the way?'

Kirk hesitated; he seemed uneasy, and he flashed a glance at Vasil Karnowski for the first time. Centre caught the glance and saw the animosity in it.

'Initially,' said John Kirk, and his accent had slipped a little under the emotion of the moment, 'they would not have wanted to tell me, for fear of upsetting me. You see, I also was in love with Magda.'

The room was silent. John Kirk's own embarrassment at admitting publicly a love he had felt over twenty years ago, for a woman who had recently died, affected everyone in the courtroom. There was something indecent in the process which dragged such an admission from the man, for it was a prying into matters that were of concern to few in that room. But that was the danger of a court action, thought Centre; it could mean that things were said that should not be said for a man's peace of mind, for his pride – and once said they became public property.

McIver's voice was completely lacking in emotion. He was in control.

'While that would be a sentiment that might dictate their actions in the first instance, it would hardly justify their silence when it was discovered that she was pregnant.'

Kirk inclined his head; his eyes were veiled.

'That is so, my lord.'

What about the jackboots? thought Centre. What about the fear and pressures of the times, the rape of Austria, the armies marching, the urgency of the Karnowskis' attempt to reach England and safety? Did all this count for nothing? And yet he had to admit to himself that it was strange that the lovers had not spoken more positively of their marriage.

Stenson was speaking.

'Let me get one thing perfectly clear, Mr Kirk. Did you regard your cousin and Magda as married?'

Kirk shrugged one shoulder; it was a peculiarly un-English gesture.

'I suppose I did.'

'And yet–'

'Please let me explain. This all happened a long time ago. For more than one reason it was a time of fear and pain … and I was young. My memory of those times is not good. All I will say is this. I always assumed that they were married ... though there remained a suspicion at the back of my mind that they were not. We did not speak of it, but they lived as man and wife and they were married to all intents and purposes. But I must, in all honesty, state that to my knowledge they never went through a ceremony of marriage. Perhaps it was just the times, and the pressures in Austria... I do not know. But I repeat, sadly, that I know of no ceremony.'

Centre knew that John Kirk wanted to help, but could not. When Karnowski was cross-examined on his affidavit the same story would no doubt emerge. So for Centre and his client it must be simply a question of a holding operation until the news came through from Austria. It was almost as though the thought were transmitted to his client, for Stephen Kirk leaned towards Centre at that moment and whispered,

'Have you heard anything from that private enquiry agent yet?'

Centre shook his head.

'Not yet. We should hear by tomorrow afternoon. I'm hoping that the lead he has will be productive. It's certainly true that the family spent three months at what would be the relevant time in Neuberg. There's a chance that we'll pick up something there.'

A remote chance. A chance that was coming up only now, late in the day, after the months of waiting for the hearing to take place, after the months of searching on the Continent.

But, thought Centre, as the proceedings drew to a close for the day, if anyone can turn up the evidence, Paul Iles will.

Mr Justice McIver was rising. It was the end of the hearing for the day. It would be resumed on Monday. This would give Centre breathing space, at least. Stenson leant over and touched his arm.

'You'll let me know as soon as you hear from Austria? Don't be afraid to break into my weekend.'

'I'll do that, and thank you.'

'See you Monday then, if not before.'

Stephen walked out with Centre. John Kirk had gone, and so had the Karnowskis. Stephen seemed detached, tied up within himself, and there were clear signs of strain on his face. He said nothing, but only came awake when he saw who was waiting outside the courtroom.

'Janet!' exclaimed Centre. 'What are you doing here?'

She shrugged, colouring a little.

'You forget, Mr Centre – I had to come up for the Williams conveyance. And I thought that since it was Friday I needn't rush back

... and I decided to come along to see how things were going. Hello, Stephen.'

He was smiling at her.

'I'm delighted to see you,' he said. 'And I'm rushing in straight away to suggest that you might like to have dinner with me before you go back to Linchester.'

Centre watched her face as she replied; her pleasure at the suggestion was patent.

'Have fun, kids,' he said drily.

'Kids!' exclaimed Janet. 'Anyone would think you're ancient!'

There was a curious undertone in the way she made the remark, but Centre ignored it, and grinned. He watched them walk off together, then he turned and hailed a taxi, to make his way to the railway station.

A great deal now depended upon Paul Iles.

2

Iles had watched Neuberg awake. He had seen yawning dogs, a few darting swallows and a parade of ducks down towards the river set the streets in motion. As the sun rose he saw a housewife behind a stick fence throw a few cabbage leaves to a rabbit. A pretty girl in a blue and red skirt swept manure off the street. Women began to gossip at the street corners and down on the quay potatoes boiled in oil-drums.

But now the town was darkening. As he walked across the bridge he caught the flash of the oars of three late-evening voyagers navigating the calmer water near the river wall, spray cover protecting their gear. He crossed the bridge and walked unhurriedly past the red-roofed hotel towards the trees on the hill. It was up there that the synagogue lay, nestling among the quiet leaves. It was there that he had an appointment with Herr Brandt.

The curator was small, old and wizened as all curators should be. He was also helpful, and only too pleased that anyone should be sufficiently interested in his records to spend three days waiting until the relevant information could be found. He offered Iles some Schnapps and with grave courtesy Iles accepted it. The old man's pleasure was obvious and he chuckled.

'It is good, *hein?*'

'Very good.'

'It is not to everyone that I make the offer of my Schnapps, young man. You know that?'

'I am honoured.'

'You are also polite. That is good. Young men today, they are often not polite. They are not prepared to allow an old man time; they forget that age slows the blood, and the intellect.'

'But increases the wisdom.'

The curator peered, smiling, into Paul Iles's battered face.

'The young also can be wise, if they – how is it the Americans say? – if they work at it!'

'I'll remember that,' said Iles, laughing.

Herr Brandt matched his laugh with a dry cackle.

'But you come not to prattle with me. You have business. My records, they have interested you; and Schneider ... the year 1939 or 1940, the place possibly the synagogue...'

He paused.

'It was burned, you know, in 1943, by the Germans. We rebuilt in 1949, but it was not the same. The people ... many are no longer here. But the records ... they at least were saved.'

'And you found an entry?'

'I did.'

The old man shuffled away to the corner of the room and returned with a heavy, leather-bound book in his gnarled hands. He placed spectacles on his nose and peered at the cracked leather, shaking his head and clucking sadly. Then he opened the book, to a page marked with a small piece of paper. His finger pointed to the entry.

'The names are here. Magda Schneider. Haren Karnowski.'

'Then they married in the synagogue?'

The old man shook his head.

'It would seem that they did not. One cannot be entirely sure, of course, for those were troubled days, but what this entry shows is that they had declared an intention to marry. The fact of the marriage, it is not recorded here. For what elsewhere. Herr Holstein will be of assistance. I can arrange you will call the certificate of the marriage you must try for him to see you tomorrow, say at ten in the morning.'

Iles frowned. Time was getting short: the hearing had already started in England and only now, at this late date, was he getting warm, getting close to the truth.

'Can I not reach Herr Holstein tonight?' he asked.

The old curator looked at him with a twisted smile.

'The eagerness and impatience of youth is not to be curbed. But who am I to deny it? I will telephone Herr Holstein if you wish, and ask him, but I fear I cannot persuade on your behalf.'

He offered Iles another Schnapps, which was accepted with alacrity. Anxious to get the job done he might be, but prepared to refuse such good liquor Iles was not. The old man shuffled off and a few moments later Iles heard him speaking in a high voice on the telephone in the other room. Iles sipped at the Schnapps. It warmed him, settled him nicely. He was conscious of being close now to what he wanted.

A few minutes later Herr Brandt shuffled back into the room and dropped heavily into his chair. He peered over his spectacles at Paul Iles.

'I am afraid, *mein Herr,* that all your eagerness will be for nothing. It would seem that Herr Holstein cannot make himself available to open up the Viktor building tonight.'

'The Viktor building?'

'It is the block of offices down near the river. It has five floors and the old records of the town are kept on one of those floors – the second, it is, as I recall. Herr Holstein has custody of such matters ... but I fear he is not available this evening. It is a dinner-party.'

Iles concealed his disappointment.

'These offices and the papers they hold – are they all public records?'

'*Nein, nein,*' the old man hastened to say. 'Many of them are simply old papers of historical interest; many have not even been filed properly. But if any certificate exists concerning the marriage of these two people with whom you are concerned it is likely that it will be discovered there. However, you will both be able to search tomorrow morning–'

'Both?'

The old man stared at him, then nodded slowly.

'It would seem that yours is the second

84

enquiry. There was one made this afternoon and a visit was made to the building. The visitor professed to be unable to find what he wanted and said he would be back tomorrow.'

'He was searching for the same marriage papers?'

'So I believe. But my old ears are not what they were, you understand. I could have heard Herr Holstein wrongly, could I not?'

On the other hand, thought Iles, as he paced down the street towards the river, the curator could have heard perfectly well. If he had, who the hell was searching for the Karnowski certificate, if it existed – and equally to the point, why?

The thought stopped him in his tracks. There could be only one other person who would want access, who would want sight of the certificate, who would want to check if it existed. The man who was claiming that Stephen Kirk was illegitimate. And if he discovered the existence of the certificate...?

The moonlight was reflected brilliantly from the surface of the quiet river as Iles crossed the bridge. He heard a low, gurgled laugh from the darkness of its overhang: lovers beside the water. His shoes made no sound as he crossed the road and moved down and along the riverside towards the modern building towering out of the old town.

The Viktor building, Herr Brandt had said.

And there it was, tall, solidly ugly, with its long range of expressionless windows facing him. Iles stood in the shadowed shop doorway across the street and stared at those windows. On the second floor of that building were kept public records. Someone had been looking at them today, searching, it would seem, for evidence of the Karnowski marriage. That person had said he could not find it, and would return.

Two questions: why did he want to see the certificate? And what would he do when he found it? Karnowski would hardly want it produced if it did exist. And there would be only one way of making sure then that it was not produced.

The searcher had said that he would return tomorrow. But what if he had already discovered it? He could not take it then, under the eyes of the staff, in the afternoon. Iles stood very still in the darkness. If the certificate existed, what was there to prevent its destruction at night?

Nothing, apart from a few locks, and walls, and possibly an electrically-operated warning alarm. None of these would pose insuperable difficulties for a strongly motivated man – one who would possibly be paid a great deal of money for the destruction of a small piece of paper.

Iles suddenly realized that it was going to be a long night.

This part of the town of Neuberg was very much a business sector and it meant that few people came and went during the hours of darkness. The street itself was silent, but there was little danger of Iles falling asleep for the cold began to finger his bones. The effect of the Schnapps had soon worn off.

But he stayed where he was because he had a premonition. There wasn't a damn thing he could do about the fact that someone else had already visited the records office, but he could certainly make sure that no one visited the place again tonight. And come the dawn Paul Iles would be waiting on the doorstep, first in the queue, waiting for a probably surprised Herr Holstein.

But it was only at two in the morning, when Iles thought that he caught a faint flash of light on the first floor of the Viktor building, that he realized that he had been too confident in his assumptions. The Viktor presented a flat, unbroken façade to the front and this he could watch easily. The building itself was part of a block, and he had assumed that there would be no back entrance as such: he now realized with a sinking heart that such assumptions were dangerous. Quickly but quietly, he crossed the street.

He had been right, in fact: there was no

back entrance. He was not gladdened by the discovery for it was with considerable anger that he realized there was a side entrance that the architects had run through to the left of the block: a narrow trade and deliveries yard, it provided good cover for nefarious entry, and the fire-escape better opportunity.

Iles went up the fire-escape like a scalded but in the circumstances commendably silent cat.

The lock on the first floor had been extracted cleanly and without effort, and completely. If there had been an alarm system, it had been dealt with more than efficiently. A quick search showed Iles the power of his reasoning: three split-core wires neatly cut, one at a time. Iles moved very carefully and very quietly through the dark doorway on to the first floor of the Viktor building. He knew now that he was dealing with a professional, and the thought did not make him happy.

His rubber-soled shoes made no sound on the bare, plastic-tiled floors. He was at the end of a long corridor, but immediately to his left was a staircase; he took the first flight, half crouching and peering upwards into the darkness.

There was no sound from above.

Iles waited for what seemed an age but eventually knew he would have to move. He might yet have the advantage of surprise, for whoever was on the floor above him would not be aware of Iles's presence, whereas Iles was certain that in one of the rooms on the second floor he would discover someone with a pocket flashlight, taut nerves, and searching fingers.

The only problem was, how long had the man been in the building?

He must have found the certificate this afternoon, seen it, and would thus know where to get it. It would surely be a matter of minutes only before he could find it again. Time was of the essence, and Iles moved swiftly up the second flight to the floor above.

Again, he was at the end of a long corridor. But this time, it was different. Each of the doors along the long blank corridor was closed but each had a glass air vent at the top. And one of these emitted the faintest of glows.

Iles moved quietly down the corridor. When he reached the door he was heading for, he realized that he was in a dilemma. The choices open to him were simple: either he waited for the intruder to come out, or he went in after him. Waiting in the corridor would be the safer course, in the sense that Iles would have the benefit of complete surprise as the man emerged. On the other hand, Iles did not know what was happening inside the room; if he went in, the chance of surprise was largely gone because the intruder would see Iles before Iles saw him. But the man inside that room could already be in the process of destroying the certificate.

Iles had to go in; he couldn't chance the destruction of the paper.

He stood outside the door, considering. The faint glow still illuminated the roof of the corridor above the door but it gave no clue as to the position of the man inside the room. Iles had no choice but to burst straight in, and hope that the intruder would be more or less in line with the door. Only in that way would Iles stand a reasonable chance of taking him by surprise. He put his hand out to the door handle. Then, taking a deep breath, Iles gripped the handle, twisted it and barged his shoulder straight into the door.

The door flew open and Iles went into the room like a wild bull into the arena. He caught a brief glimpse of a torchlight on a paper-strewn desk and something dark moving towards the left, with a gasping startled sound, and then he skidded against a filing cabinet as a forearm caught him high across the cheek. He spun against the wall, catching his elbow painfully, and his arm went numb as the nerve ends jolted their protest, but he was too busy taking evasive action to care. For he had made a mistake; he had assumed there would be one intruder only.

There were two.

The man who had been at the desk was leaping swiftly across the room towards Iles; the other, who had been stationed to one side of the door, was already grabbing at the enquiry agent's throat. Iles flailed desperately with his arms, and the fingers of his left hand grabbed a handful of hair. Without hesitation, Iles drove his right hand at the target of the man's face, and the heel of his hand caught the man under the nose, throwing him back across the room with a grunt of pain. Almost immediately, it was Iles's turn to grunt as the second intruder cannoned into his chest and he went over backwards, sliding downwards against the wall.

Iles attempted to retain his balance, braced against the wall, but his attacker had taken him around the waist, pulling him downwards. Painfully aware that once he was on the floor there would be little to save him, Iles fought at the man, hitting him about the head and shoulders, frantically trying to break free before his first assailant recovered from the numbing shock of the blow he had received to the face and returned to the fray. The grip around Iles's waist slackened as Iles's fist connected behind the man's ear, but it was a momentary respite only as the first assailant staggered back in the dim light and took Iles across the cheekbone with a swinging right hand. Iles lurched sideways and collapsed, dazedly, and the man gripping him around the waist released him. Together they fell to the floor, and Iles was pinned in a corner formed by the wall and the filing cabinets as hands and legs struggled across him, and up across his chest. Fingers fastened on his throat.

He was spreadeagled. There was a knee on his chest, pressing hard just above his solar plexus and driving the air from his lungs. But worse were the fingers, cutting like wire bands into his windpipe and effectively preventing any intake of air. Iles was vaguely aware of a guttural voice, and shuffling feet: the second intruder, anxious to assist. But the man on Iles's chest didn't need assistance just at that moment: he was in control.

Iles beat at the air – he couldn't reach the man's face. He attempted to roll but the filing cabinet restricted his movement. It shook slightly, nevertheless, and something fell from the top – a heavy book. It caught Iles a painful blow across the forehead and the fingers banded around his throat moved instinctively as the object struck the man's wrist.

It was the reflex action, the momentary weakening that was all Iles needed. His eyes were squeezed tight, and his ears singing, but as those fingers weakened he seized his chance. He drove both hands up inside the wrists of his assailant: the man's arms opened fractionally, bending at the elbows, and as he did so Iles jerked his head up and forward. The objective was the man's face, and the combined effect of Iles's movements succeeded – his head collided straight with his assailant's face and Iles heard the man's nose crack as it came into contact with the top of Iles's skull.

The pressure was gone from his throat, and the man on Iles's chest sagged sideways, moaning, but there was no respite for the enquiry agent. His own head was buzzing as he thrust the man aside and attempted to get from under the sagging weight of his assailant, but then there was a boot taking him under the heart, and again driving every ounce of breath out of his body. His eyes stared upwards and he caught the dark shadow of the man on his feet driving forward again with a violent kick before he twisted away. A sharp pain scored the underside of his arm as he rolled, but a third kick would be coming.

Iles rolled again, over the man on the floor, now struggling to rise, and he felt something under his hand. The heavy book, which had fallen from the filing cabinet. Even as the boot drove at him for a third time Iles threw the book, with all the strength that he could muster, straight at the head of the dark shadow above him.

He missed by a yard. The boot took him in the stomach, glancing up towards his ribs and there was an appalling, shattering crash. Iles wondered through a haze of pain how it was that ribs could make such a noise, and then he was lying back in a daze as someone grunted, and rasped heavily for breath. Then the light was gone and darkness drifted in.

He must have been lying there fighting for breath for at least two minutes. Gradually his eyes focused in the darkness. He was alone. He got to his feet gingerly, gripping the edge of the desk to rise, and he felt the current of cold air on his face, cold night air, and he realized what had happened. The book he had thrown had gone straight through the window. It was the glass he had heard shatter, not his ribs. And the intruders couldn't take the chance of further discovery – the broken window and the possibility of assistance for Iles had put them to flight. And from the aches in his body, and the muzziness of his head, thought Iles, not a moment too soon. Awkwardly, he sank into the chair behind the paper-strewn desk. He fumbled in the darkness for the telephone. Heroism was no longer fashionable. Heroism was out. Time to call the police.

3

It was on Sunday night that the telephone in David Centre's flat rang. It was a long-distance call, from Neuberg. It was Paul Iles. Centre wasted no time in preliminaries.

'Iles – have you got it?'

Iles's tone sounded aggrieved.

'I've got every damn thing! Contusions about the face, fingerprints on my neck, multiple bruises on my ribs and stomach, a very painful, deep scratch along the underside of one arm, and one very good and very expensive shirt which is torn, bloody and in every way ruined.'

'What the hell has been going on?'

'Well, let's put it like this. It looks as though someone else wanted to get hands on the certificate before your client could.'

Centre was silent for a moment.

'I don't understand,' he said slowly. Iles was only too pleased to give his reading of the situation.

'There's only one person who would want to get hold of the paper. Karnowski. If you want my view, what's happened is this. He knew that Haren and Magda might have married, or did marry, in Neuberg but he wasn't sure if the marriage took place or was registered. He'd be prepared to leave well alone unless I got close to it. He must have been checking on my activities, and once I began to sniff in the direction of the Neuberg synagogue he got some local characters to check for him at the Viktor building. They found the certificate, but couldn't do anything then and there, so they went back under cover of darkness. Fortunately, I was close too, then, and like a clown I barged in on them. We had something of a roughhouse. I only trust that they're as sore as I am, because then they'll be as unhappy as I am.'

'Did they destroy the paper?'

'Well, it was like this. The clerks had not returned the books to their proper places and these characters had some difficulty in finding the right one. They were still looking when I arrived. Now me, my instincts are sounder than theirs. I found the thing straight away.'

'What did you do with it?'

'Actually,' Iles said blandly, 'I threw it out of the window.'

'You what?'

'Don't worry about it. When the police arrived with Herr Holstein and we searched and couldn't find the book I thought it had been taken, but then one of the local *polizei* came in with this book that I'd heaved out and there it was, all safe, sound and prettily written.'

'But why on earth did you throw–'

'It's a long story. I'll tell you all about it when I submit my claim for expenses. It might soften you into accepting my inflated fees.'

'But you managed to get a copy of the entry?'

'I did. It was sent express this morning.'

'What about these people you found in the building?'

'Not much that can be done.' There was regret in Iles's voice. 'The local police can't help and I didn't even see either of the villains. There's a chance that they might pick up the one whose nose I broke – did I hear you wince?'

'But even if he is found, do you think we'll be able to link him to Karnowski?'

'I have my doubts. Anyway, seems to me that the main thing is that they didn't get rid of the entry, and the certificate is on its way.'

'Does it constitute the evidence we want?'

'Hell, Mr Centre, I'm no lawyer, and the damn thing's in German and all that's up to you and your witnesses, isn't it? Still, if there's nothing more now I'll ring off. Mission over, I'm flying back tomorrow morning. Been at the police headquarters in Neuberg all damn day convincing them I'm basically honest and above board.'

'All right, Iles, I'll see you when you get back. And … well, thanks.'

'My bruises respond beautifully to the

sentiment. Be seeing you.'

Centre replaced the receiver. A certain sense of excitement flickered in his veins and he felt that he needed to celebrate in a way, now that the certificate relating to the Karnowski marriage had been located. And yet he realized also that they were a long way from getting out of the wood yet. That certificate would have to be validated, and that could be a hurdle in itself. As soon as it arrived he'd have to get it sent to an expert witness.

And Karnowski. It could only be Karnowski who had engaged agents to break into the Neuberg building. But then, there was a lot at stake – the Kirk inheritance. For Karnowski, a shipping clerk in London, it could mean no stopping at desperate measures. Stephen Kirk could be regarded as damned lucky that Iles had got there in time.

Suddenly David Centre began to prowl around the flat. There were occasions when this mood took him, when a sense of depression washed over him. His flat was comfortable enough, consisting of a sitting-room, a kitchen and breakfast-room, a small dining-room and one bedroom, with a bathroom leading off the narrow corridor, but there were occasions when it was a most unsatisfying place to be. It was situated in Canynge Square, just off the main road, and the dull muted hum of traffic was sometimes obtrusive in the evening as Centre sat reading, or watching the flickering television Westerns that drew him in fascinated boredom.

He had not been able to place with any precision the reasons why the flat was occasionally unsatisfying, for all that. He had blamed the traffic, but it was not the traffic alone; he had blamed Linchester, the quality of the night life, the pawkiness of the streets around the square, the confining size of the flat, the narrowness of his existence, but it was none of these things, in essence. It was something else, something more basic perhaps, something more essential.

Perhaps it was the flat expanse of the St Lawrence and the drift of the Rockies to the sky, the shouts of the engineers on the Seaway, lost in a void of silence and a morass of struggling mud. There were times when he remembered those days with what almost amounted to a physical ache in his chest. There was the memory of the blue 'goop' – the greasy clay that came sloshing out of the dredge buckets and which, exposed to the air and sun, turned rubbery or brittle until a shower turned it to thick soup again. There was the time when the engineers had to dispense with compressed air drills and shoot jets of flame into the stone, at five times the speed of sound. There was the cold in the river valley – twenty-five and thirty-five degrees below zero and metal objects burned to the touch, gear assemblies stiffened so that lubrication was impossible and drivers were forced to free tractor treads with blow-torches. Concrete froze before it could set...

In those days there had been a rawness, a harshness and a violence about life that left him no time for the privacy of thought. No time, nor inclination. But Linchester was a world away from the Seaway. Here he was in a new professional environment, among new people, and new problems. Not his own; other people's problems. Other people, like Stephen Kirk.

But there were times when the confining walls of his flat were too narrow, when his soul wanted to stretch, when he wanted to remember how it had been with his wife, with the moonlight on his face... It was this that made him take the Aston Martin out of Linchester, to drive past the row of houses into the quiet, ringing hills above the sprawl of lights that was Linchester. From Sault Hill he could see for forty miles, or imagine in the darkness that he could. There were other cars here; courting couples. He sat quietly in the Aston Martin and watched the darkness and saw the small glow in the sky above Sandhill. He remembered another place and saw in his mind's eye the saw-toothed mountains and the way the sun had burst up, lancing sharp fingers of light into the valleys, but he hadn't been alone then, as he was now.

He shrugged the thought aside. His wife was dead; those days were dead. This was now and there was just the empty seat beside him, and the warm summer darkness and the faint red glow in the sky above Sandhill.

That glow would have been brighter, the night that Harry and Magda Kirk had died.

He turned the car and drove back into Linchester. He needed a drink.

He went to the lounge bar in the Callender Hotel, the pretentious building in the main street just off the square. He went there because he wanted the comfortable babble of conversation in which he need not join; he wanted solitude among a group of people, silence in the midst of chatter. Instead, he found the lounge empty but for about five people, and two of them, sitting together, were Stephen Kirk and Janet Sanders.

'Well, hello, Mr Centre – I didn't think you were let out at night!'

Janet was smiling as she called out to him, but there was a strange confusion in her eyes. Centre was pressed to join them, and it would have been impolite to refuse but he vowed silently to get away as quickly as possible.

'May I get you a drink?'

'Like a shot,' said Janet, and Stephen

quickly finished his whisky at Centre's invitation. Centre brought the gin, whisky and his own glass of beer to their table.

'And your very good health' said Stephen tritely, sipping at the whisky.

'You seem tired,' remarked Janet, looking at Centre carefully.

He shook his head, smiling.

'Just my age, compared with yours. Bags under the eyes and all that.'

'Rubbish! You'll be making out that you're old enough to be my father next. And you're not a day over thirty-five.'

'Don't fish. Just because I have the advantage of knowing your age.'

'How come?' Stephen's query sounded innocent.

'Application to join the firm.'

'Anything else on the application?'

'Lots. What do you want to know?'

'I don't care for this conversation,' Janet said. 'You're discussing me as though I were a horse. You'll be wanting to see my teeth next.'

'Or something!' Stephen was giggling and Centre looked briefly at him; the man was strangely juvenile at times.

'By the way,' Centre said, 'I heard from Paul Iles, the enquiry agent, early this evening. It would seem that he's got what we want. Evidence of a ceremony of marriage between Harry and Magda.'

102

Stephen's eyes were wide.

'You mean—'

'Now wait a minute! I said evidence of a ceremony of marriage. That doesn't mean we're out of the wood yet. We've still to prove it was a valid marriage, and that's where our expert witness will come in. But at least it's a gleam of light.'

'I'm still surprised,' said Janet, 'that they didn't tell John Kirk and Karnowski about the ceremony. At the time, I mean.'

'Perhaps they did,' suggested Stephen, glowering.

'But—'

'Well, it's true that perhaps Cousin John wasn't told, or maybe he forgets it – he was young, and it was a long time ago. But Vasil Karnowski – I think he must have known. But he has kept it to himself, hoping it wouldn't come to light.'

'Don't bank too heavily on it, Stephen,' said Centre carefully. 'We don't know that the certificate, when it comes, will strongly support our case. We haven't seen it yet.'

Stephen sat staring at his drink. He made no reply. There was some desultory small talk between Janet and Centre, which was notable for its uncharacteristic brittleness: the relationship that they enjoyed in the office was not carried over socially, it would seem. Janet seemed nervous, and was in the end constrained to talk about work.

'By the way, Mr Centre, Mr Chambers has been ringing. He wants an appointment early next week.'

'Chambers? Oh yes, Don Chambers. Did he say what it was about?'

'Something about conveyancing work.'

Centre pondered. The Karnowski suit was taking up a great deal of his time, but he had a living to earn outside that affair. Chambers had spoken to him once before, since he had defended him on the driving charge, concerning the appeal that the police were making against Chambers's acquittal. At that time he had mentioned that he might be putting some lucrative business Centre's way.

'All right, Janet, will you try to fix an appointment for Tuesday? I'll be up at Chancery on Monday for the hearing, but we might have to ask for an adjournment, so Tuesday for Chambers would be suitable.'

He glanced towards Stephen Kirk to apologize for 'talking shop', but was surprised to see that the young man could hardly have been aware of the conversation he was having with Janet. Stephen was looking, quite fixedly, at his drink. He seemed oblivious of the presence of either of them.

Even as Centre glanced quickly towards Janet, Stephen rose to his feet, brushing a hand across his forehead as though to push back the errant lock of dark hair.

'Will you excuse me for a moment. I … I'll be back shortly … something I must do.'

Janet's eyes widened, and she opened her mouth as though to say something, but then thought better of it. Stephen left the table and walked out through the door. Centre, in a little embarrassment, sipped at the last inch of beer in his glass. After a short silence, Janet said,

'I thought you would be a whisky man.'

'I had no doubt that you would be a gin woman.'

The easiness of their office relationship was suddenly back between them. Had it been the presence of Stephen Kirk that had inhibited them?

'That just shows how wrong you are, really. I'm not a gin woman at all, it's just that I thought that since my boss was paying I might as well cane him for what I could get. Normally I just drink tonic water.'

'How you have the nerve to cane me, as you put it, when the firm is in such a parlous state, I can't imagine. I shall watch you drink that gin and regard it as liquid profits vanishing down your throat.'

It was a pretty throat.

'Parlous state!' she mocked. 'The way clients are coming in, and being dealt with by Charles Blake, you'll either have to raise his salary or get an assistant solicitor in the firm.'

'Yes. I've been thinking about that... I've also been thinking that you'll have to give up the reception work.'

'Things aren't *that* hectic in the outer office!'

'Maybe not, but the filing is getting difficult. I think I'll have to ask you to work as my secretary, Janet, full time, with a new receptionist in the outer office. You can work in the small room across from mine and we'll link up an inter-communicating system. You'll be adjoining Blake's room so that he can get hold of you easily too–'

'You could have phrased *that* more delicately!'

'–and we both need someone reliable to take work off our hands. I'll pay you a larger salary, of course.'

'You are trying to corrupt me!'

He caught her glance.

'Hardly that,' he replied solemnly.

'I accept,' she said, with equal gravity.

Silence fell between them, but a silence far more companionable than the conversation when Stephen had been with them. Centre looked around.

'Where *is* your boy-friend?'

'I wish you wouldn't speak so loosely. For a lawyer it's a bad habit. But I agree – where is Stephen? Hadn't you better look for him?'

He eyed her uncertainly. She smiled.

'*I* can hardly do so,' she said.

Centre returned five minutes later.

'I've looked in the other bars, the telephone booths, and those places where young ladies are denied entry–'

'The gents', you mean.'

'That's right,' Centre admitted with a grin. 'He's nowhere to be seen. Your charming young man has skipped.'

'He's *not* my young man.'

'Your companion.'

'That's better.'

'Which, I suppose, leaves me holding the baby.'

'You really should watch your language.'

'You really shouldn't be so literal.'

'My dear Mr Centre, for as long as I can remember – at least, since I was sixteen, and that's as far back as anyone should want to remember – boys have been telling me that what they had in mind was not what I'd thought at all. But I prefer to be literal about words, and deeds too for that matter. As for young Stephen Kirk, I'll take his defection literally and haul him over the coals, sweetly of course, when next we meet. In the meanwhile–'

She picked up her handbag. She was wearing a plain high-necked sweater which was sleeveless, and a dark green skirt. She was hardly dressed to kill. Nevertheless, David Centre thought that she looked very attractive. He would not have dreamed of telling her so, particularly when she looked at him in that direct way of hers, with the glint of humour in her brown eyes.

'I'll walk you home.'

'You don't need to.'

'I know. I will anyway.'

'It's not done, a solicitor walking his receptionist home.'

'Not even if she's about to become his secretary? Come on, let's go.'

The evening had changed its flavour. When he had driven back from Sault Hill it had been with a sense of depression, but now he felt warm and the warmth was occasioned by Janet's company. They walked down the main street, past the lighted shopping centre of Linchester, and Janet motioned the direction that they should take. They paused once or twice as Janet stopped to look into a shop window but they said very little to each other. She seemed to be enjoying the comfortable silence as much as he.

Beyond the town centre the road was darker and they turned on to the estate where Janet lived with her parents. To his query, she replied, 'I've got a brother and two sisters. Bill, my brother, works in Ealing – we don't see a great deal of him. My sisters – well, they're twins and they'll be doing their O levels next year. Dad? He works for British Rail: stationmaster.'

The house was semi-detached, unpretentious, carefully kept.

'Would you like to come in for a cup of coffee?'

'Thank you, Janet, I think not. I'll say good night, and get back home.'

'As you like.'

He made no move to go and an awkward silence fell between them. For some strange reason Centre felt that he should say something to end their brief evening together but there was nothing to say, and it would be absurd to shake her hand. The thought disturbed him in a way he couldn't understand – why should the thought of touching her disturb him?

'You're not English, are you, Mr Centre?'

He smiled.

'Oh yes, I am. The Canadian inflections put it in doubt, I know, but I was born in England, and indeed went to school in the West Country. But my parents emigrated to Canada: I was out there with them after I left school at sixteen.'

'Did you practise law in Canada?'

'No. My father was an engineer. He was rather keen that I should follow in his line but I couldn't agree with him. I ended up in articles and became a surveyor. Qualified when I was twenty-one and then travelled around on various projects. Spent some time on the St Lawrence Seaway, around 1957.'

'You've an unusual background for a lawyer.'

'I know,' he agreed. 'It's not often one changes horses in mid-stream as I did. The fact is ... I found life in Canada not to my choosing. I pulled up stakes and came back to England. The law appealed to me; I'd saved some money, and my father helped. I got articles in the Midlands, spent a short period as an assistant solicitor after I qualified, and then ... Linchester.'

'Is your wife still in Canada, Mr Centre?'

In the semi-darkness he couldn't see Janet's face very clearly, and it was half averted anyway.

'How did you know I'd been married?'

'Intuition.'

He made no reply to that and after a moment she turned away.

'I'm sorry, Mr Centre. I shouldn't have asked that – it's none of my business.'

'No, Janet, I was just thinking. I don't mind your asking. Don't interpret my silence as my having taken offence. My wife ... well, she died about five years ago.'

'I still shouldn't have asked.'

'Natural curiosity. Anyway, look, there's a light on upstairs. Your parents must be going to bed. If you don't go in, you might get locked out.'

'I *am* over twenty-one!'

He detected some exasperation in her tone

and he chuckled.

'Only just,' he countered. 'Good night, Janet.'

4

Vasil Karnowski gave his evidence on Monday morning. In many ways it was a stereotype of John Kirk's statements. Except that it was more positive, more malicious, more motivated. Vasil Karnowski was not inhibited by affection for Magda, or sympathy for Stephen. He knew what he was after and he was determined to get it. He left no doubt in the minds of counsel or Mr Justice McIver that he was absolutely convinced that Haren Karnowski had never married Magda Schneider.

But that, thought Centre to himself, is where you might well be wrong. He had received the certificate from Iles – or at least a copy of it. It was now in the hands of an expert witness for the defence, and a second copy had this morning been handed to Warrender, Karnowski's counsel. They would try to cast doubt upon its validity, of course.

During Monday afternoon a certain Robert Penry, a former employee of Kirk's, and witness for the prosecution, was cross-examined on his affidavit.

'Mr Penry,' said Stenson smoothly, 'you state in your affidavit that Haren Kirk told you quite categorically that Stephen was a bastard.'

'He did.'

Robert Penry settled his hands, linking his fingers together. He was a burly man, with a deep-lined face and thick lips that he touched occasionally with a flickering tongue.

'He said this in so many words?'

'Yes.'

'What words?'

'Well, he simply said that he was a bastard.'

'You were a confidant of Haren Kirk?'

'No I was employed by him.'

'In what capacity?'

'I was works manager up at the Grangetown factory. Had been ever since the factory opened.'

'I see. And according to your affidavit, this statement relating to … ah … bastardy was made, let me see, almost seven years ago.'

'Yes.'

'You remember well.'

'I do.'

'What was so special about that occasion that you would remember this statement after such a lapse of time?'

'Something happened just about then.'

'I think, Mr Penry, we'd like to hear about it.'

'Well, there had been some sort of panic on at Grangetown. Harry Kirk came around in a hell of a tear because the books at Grangetown had been cooked, you know? He came storming into my office and had a go at me, but of course I soon showed him I had no control over the financial side of things. But he worried me and he had the auditors in for weeks.'

'And?'

'Well, in the end he pulled his ... his son Stephen out of Grangetown, and as far as I understand, sent him packing. Seemed to blame him for something or other connected with the cooking of the books. Anyway, next day he came in to see me. That's when he said it.'

'What did he say?'

'Well, something like– "That's how he treats me, the bastard. That's how he treats me, for all the work I have put in, the way I have built up the firm for him, the little bastard. That is what he is, Penry, a little bastard." It was like that he spoke, well, not quite like that, for he had a bit of an accent you know, being a Pole and angry and all that.'

'I see.'

Stenson paused for a moment as though weighing his words with care.

'Mr Penry, up at your factory in Grangetown, what would happen if someone called you a bastard?'

Penry glowered.

'I'd plant one on him!'

'You mean you'd strike him?'

'I'd snap him in two.'

'Why?'

Penry looked confused.

'Why? Well, you know, it's not a nice thing to say about a man!'

'Because it places your parentage in doubt?'

'Eh? Well, no, but–'

'Or because it is a recognized term of abuse?'

'Well, I suppose that's–'

'For isn't that what Harry Kirk was saying, seven years ago? Wasn't he merely indulging in factory floor abuse? Wasn't he furious over some incident involving his son, hadn't he just thrown him out of the factory, wasn't he railing at him, calling him names, abusing him verbally? Wasn't' that all it was? Mere verbal abuse?'

Penry's tongue flickered wildly over his lips.

'Well, I...'

He hesitated, but then went no further. After a short silence Mr Justice McIver leaned forward.

'I think you have made your point, Mr Stenson. Cross-examination over – re-examine, Mr Warrender?'

'But two swallows,' Stenson said tritely later in the day as he and Centre left the court, 'don't make a summer. You've put the certificate to Mr Strougal, our foreign expert witness?'

'I have,' replied Centre. 'He'll be ready to be called on Wednesday or Thursday. I take it that Karnowski's case will be rested then?'

'Oh, I think so. He'll attack the certificate with his expert witness early Wednesday morning, I imagine. You know, I suspect that everything will rest on that piece of paper.'

'I just hope that it will stand up,' said Centre fervently. It was a thought that bothered him most of the way back to Linchester.

Next morning he had other things to think about.

'You have an appointment with Mr Chambers for ten this morning, Mr Centre,' said Janet as he entered the office. He nodded, and walked through to have a word with Blake to see how things were going, and then went into his own room to deal with an accumulation of mail. There were three conveyances to be checked before he passed them through to Blake for completion, and he was still immersed with them when Janet buzzed him on the intercom to tell him that Mr Chambers had arrived.

Don Chambers advanced into the room with his hand outstretched.

'Good to see you again, Centre. Been a few months, hasn't it? Sorry I've not been in touch before really, but you know how things are. How's the police appeal going?'

'Over your acquittal for the driving offence? I think it will be dealt with shortly now; you should be hearing from me about it quite soon.'

'Good.'

Chambers dropped his bulk heavily into a chair and deposited on the floor the rolled paper he carried under his arm. He ran a hard hand through his fair hair and squinted up at Centre.

'Last time I spoke to you I hinted I'd be putting some business your way. Well, I am. You know the Eltham Estate? Small three-and four-bedroomed, detached and semi-detached. Prices ranging from £5500 to £9750, but still climbing fast. I'm building on about thirty lots down there. I want you to handle the conveyancing.'

'I see. That shouldn't be a problem.'

'Problem!' Chambers exclaimed. 'Come on, Centre, you can do better than that. Be a bit more bloody effusive! I know how you solicitor chaps work. Those thirty plots are all part of the old Eltham land, and they'll all be based on the same root of title. The demand for housing in this area is such that those plots will be snapped up and you'll be getting fees for thirty conveyances with a minimum of work. I know you'll search for each, but even so–'

'Even so, it's a useful amount of work to be sure of coming in.'

'Right! That's settled then – you act for Don Chambers in the matter of the Eltham Estate.'

He slumped back in the chair and stared at Centre in appreciation.

'I like you, lad, I liked the way you handled that police court case, and I like your style. You're cool, you know, you don't ruffle. You've impressed me. That's why I'm cutting you in on even a thicker slice of cake.'

'Cake?'

'Sandhill Down.'

He made a gesture of dismissal with his hand.

'Eltham Estate is peanuts. I've got bigger stuff to deal with. Sandhill Down is something I've been trying to get my teeth into for three years, and now it looks as though I'm going to get them sunk in good and deep. It's why I've come to live down here anyway. It's a big deal, Centre.'

He pointed towards the rolled paper on the floor.

'If I can get the right sort of financial backing – and it looks now as though I'm going to get it – there will be a tremendous development in the wind for Sandhill Down. I'll be shifting a million and a half quid, that's for sure.'

Something stirred at the back of Centre's mind, and he frowned.

'Sandhill Down... Will you get the relevant planning permission for the area? I seem to remember...'

That was it; Alderman Lorey's speech, the night Centre had been at the Law Society dinner.

'I'll get planning permission,' said Chambers shortly. 'Take my word for it. And like I said, when I get it, and with the right backing, I'll be shifting a mint. And you, lad, will be sharing in it. Because you'll be acting for me in all that beautiful conveyancing.'

'Things are looking up at Gordon Street!'

Chambers laughed and began to unroll the map.

'That's what I like about you, Centre, you're so bloody enthusiastic about everything!'

5

The Chief Inspector looked at the detective-sergeant and his eyes were cold. The sergeant shivered.

'Why,' asked the Chief Inspector with precision, 'did you take it upon yourself to go to

Kirkley Hall after the coroner had declared the deaths to be accidental?'

The sergeant shrugged unhappily.

'I … I still felt … I had a sort of hunch that there was more to it than that, sir.'

'And you had said that in your opinion the lab people should have been brought in. You said that in your report to me, as I remember. And I overruled you. Yet you still visited Kirkley Hall again.'

'Yes, sir … and found the hip flask, sir.'

The Chief Inspector's eyebrows drew together at the note of defiance that had crept into the sergeant's last words.

'Tell me, Sergeant,' he said, 'what did you find on that flask?'

'Nothing, sir,' said the sergeant, somewhat crestfallen, but still not browbeaten. 'And that's the funny thing, sir.'

'Go on.'

'A fire at Kirkley Hall, sir, and two people dead. Then I find a hip flask, which the lab confirms has been used to carry paraffin. And that flask is clean as a whistle – not one smudge of a fingerprint. *Wiped* clean, sir.'

'So?'

'Don't you find it curious, sir?'

The Chief Inspector smiled thinly.

'As a matter of fact, Sergeant, I do. Particularly since I had a second visitor this afternoon. A certain Mr Lawson. Who had some rather interesting things to say in addition to what we've already heard from another source. Perhaps you would care to read his statement, Sergeant.'

The Chief Inspector walked across to the window and stood looking out at the gathering darkness while the sergeant read silently at his back. After a few minutes he turned, and the sergeant looked up.

'It would seem,' said the Chief Inspector quietly, 'that you were in the right in the first instance. So I want you out there tonight with two men. I want a thorough search made of the place. And anything you find will be turned over to the forensic liaison officer for the lab people to deal with. Understood?'

'Yes, sir.'

'Then get on with it; we've waited long enough.'

Which, he thought to himself, was a sufficiently unjustified remark to make the young sergeant, smarting under the injustice of it, really pull his finger out.

There were two sergeants and two constables out at Kirkley Hall that evening. But it was during the following evening that they found what they wanted. Both sergeants were in the house when they heard the constable call. They ran out into the drive and found him at the garage doors. He led them inside, explained what had happened, and they flashed their torches around, searching the garage thoroughly.

In the corner, under a pile of sacking, they found it. A can of paraffin, half-empty. And a pile of paraffin-soaked rags.

6

Lockwood had brought in a man from Cambridge, Hensak, as expert witness for Karnowski and when Warrender took him through his evidence they were all there to hear it – Vasil and Elaine Karnowski, John Kirk sitting disdainfully apart from his brother, Stephen nervous and a little distraught. Warrender's tones carried confidently around the courtroom.

'Will you begin, Professor Hensak, by telling us your particular qualifications and experience for speaking on these present issues?'

Hensak was a small, bird-like man with large spectacles from behind which he peered ineffectively. He complied quickly with Warrender's request, and as he spoke his hands made odd fluttering motions.

'But certainly. I am Polish by birth. I practised law in Poland, quite extensively, until 1932. In that year I took up a university appointment. After three years I left on a visiting fellowship to the United States as lecturer in comparative law and then a year

later I came to England on a similar appointment. In 1965 I became Professor of
Comparative Law. My special interest has
been Conflict of Laws. I am particularly
conversant with the position concerning
Polish and German law.'

'Thank you, Professor. Now you have seen
copies of the affidavits. Before I ask you to
comment on the situation, and upon the so-
called certificate which has been handed to
you, I will first ask – if the question of the
formal validity of a marriage arises, what
law is to be applied in deciding that
question?'

Hensak fluttered his hands.

'Without doubt, the *lex loci celebrationis* –
that is, the law of the place where the
marriage was celebrated.'

'I see. In this case, according to the ... ah
... certificate, it would be–'

'Austria.'

'Now tell me, Professor. If the so-called
marriage is no marriage in the place where
it is celebrated?'

'Then it is no marriage anywhere.'

'Irrespective of the domicile of the parties?'

'That is of no consequence in the issue.
The marriage must be formally valid according to the *lex loci celebrationis.*'

'Thank you. Now perhaps you would be
good enough to look again at the document
that you hold in your hand.'

'It is the certificate – or, rather, an attested copy of the certificate – that speaks of a marriage between Haren Karnowski and Magda Schneider.'

'Would you wish to offer an opinion on that document?'

'Opinion?' hissed Stephen Kirk in Centre's ear. 'I thought witnesses had to testify as to fact, not opinion!'

Centre turned his head slightly and murmured in reply, 'There is an exception in the case of expert witnesses; they testify as to opinion. It's a recognized rule.'

Hensak was staring at the document in his hand. Warrender repeated the question.

'Would you offer an opinion on that document?'

Hensak shrugged.

'In my considered view it is of no validity whatsoever. It cannot be considered as proof of the existence of a valid marriage!'

Warrender smiled grimly. Centre glanced across to Karnowski: the predatory head was pushed forward eagerly. Beyond him Centre could see Stephen's other cousin, John Kirk. He looked pale.

'Perhaps,' said Warrender smoothly, 'you would enlarge upon that statement, Professor. Why would you disregard this as proof?'

Hensak smiled weakly, and fluttered his pale hands.

'The so-called certificate is simply a statement of facts shown in a register kept in a synagogue in Austria. It does not of itself constitute a marriage certificate in the strict, evidential sense. But this is largely irrelevant, in any case. The fact is that this paper states that two people went through a ceremony of marriage at a particular date, time and place. It is supported by an affidavit from the officating cantor. Little weight can be attached to either document.'

'And–?'

'And in any case, at that time, 1940, Austria was subject to the German Marriage Law of 1938.'

Warrender smiled.

'What is the effect of that law?'

'Under Austrian law in 1940, in accordance with the German Marriage Law, a ceremony of marriage celebrated in a church or synagogue will be of no effect. The law demanded a civil ceremony for there to be a valid marriage.'

'A civil ceremony! And do these certificates show the existence of a civil ceremony?'

'They do not. A ceremony in the synagogue only. That is not good enough. Legally the parties were not married. The marriage was formally invalid.'

Centre heard Stephen Kirk's hissed intake of breath. He glanced at the young man; Stephen was showing signs of distress –

there was perspiration on his forehead and his eyes were suddenly vacant. Centre touched his shoulder in sympathy.

Stenson was rising to cross-examine.

'Professor Hensak, you say that you left Poland and eventually came to England for a lecturing post. Have you ever practised law in Germany?'

'No, but–'

'Or in Austria?'

'No. I was about to say–'

'But you have considerable lecturing experience in comparative law, and you will also, of course, have dealt with conflicts involving German, Austrian, and Polish law.'

'Certainly.'

'But you haven't practised anywhere but Poland; you are an academic.'

'That is right.'

'Would you say that one is an adequate substitute for the other?'

'I do not follow the question.'

'Would you say that academic expertise is an adequate substitute for professional experience?'

Hensak glowered. He was saved by Mr Justice McIver.

'Mr Stenson – I trust that you are not proceeding in this cross-examination in an attempt to show that Professor Hensak cannot be regarded as an expert. You will be aware that the question as to whether a proposed witness is properly qualified is decided by the Bench as a condition precedent to the admissibility of the evidence. I shall simply emphasize that I have already ruled the evidence admissible.'

Stenson smiled; he was an elegant man, with a charming smile.

'That was not my intention, my lord. I waive the question.'

But Centre knew that the point had been made. Stenson had thrown doubt upon Hensak's qualities and qualifications – which was all that was necessary in view of what was coming. It came when Stenson called the expert witness for Stephen Kirk, on the Thursday afternoon.

'Mr Strougal, would you please tell the court what *your* experience and qualifications are?'

Strougal adjusted his huge bulk. His voice was deep, his accent a combination of foreign and BBC.

'For ten years I have been acting in an official capacity in the Austrian embassy in London, and I have practised as jurist consult in commercial cases involving Austrian law. For ten years before the War I was an advocate in Austria and held a part-time lecturing post in Vienna. I still hold a practising certificate.'

'Your lecturing – was it in Austrian law or comparative law?'

'Austrian law.'

'You would describe yourself as a practitioner rather than as an academic?'

Strougal looked surprised that the thought should ever have been expressed.

'Most certainly.'

'I could ask you whether you consider teaching is an adequate substitute for practice, Mr Strougal, but I will not embarrass you. What I will ask is this. You have heard the evidence given by the expert witness, Professor Hensak. Do you have any comment to make upon his findings?'

'Only – without wishing to detract in any way from his academic competence – that he speaks arrant nonsense.'

In the utter silence that fell upon the courtroom Centre could see Vasil Karnowski sitting bolt upright. John Kirk also had lost his disdain for the proceedings and was leaning forward in keen interest. Stephen was still at Centre's side.

'Ah,' breathed Stenson. 'Now why should you be so dogmatic, Mr Strougal?'

'Because Profession Hensak has both misread the document in question, and also has overlooked an important provision in the Austrian laws promulgated in 1945.'

Stenson smiled thinly.

'Perhaps you would take us through the situation, Mr Strougal, treating each point in turn.'

'Certainly. The parties went through a ceremony of marriage in 1940. It is perfectly true, as Professor Hensak says, that only a civil ceremony would validate the marriage under the 1938 Act. But he errs thereafter.'

He took a deep breath.

'In the first instance he states that the certificate is only a statement of facts kept in a register in a synagogue. That is not correct. It is not a marriage certificate; this I agree to be the case. But it is not a document kept in a synagogue. He has misunderstood the position. It is a record of a marriage *celebrated* in a synagogue – *but it is a record kept in the public registry office.*'

'Your inflection suggests that this is a point of some importance.'

'Quite so. For the second point upon which Professor Hensak errs in this. While it is true that the German Marriage law of 1938 applied in 1940, the situation changed in 1945. The Germans were expelled from Austria and in June of 1945 a special law was passed providing that religiously celebrated marriages would be retrospectively validated, provided that they were registered in an appropriate public register.'

'Would you explain the importance of this?'

'The importance must be obvious. The parties went through a religious ceremony of marriage. A civil ceremony they did not enter into. At that time, in 1940, this was not enough. The marriage was therefore formally invalid. But they *had* registered the marriage in the public registry, and the fact that it was so registered meant that the marriage was caught up by the Act of 1945, and *retrospectively validated.*'

'So that if one looked at the marriage, say, in 1950, what would the decision be, in an Austrian court?'

'The decision would be that the marriage was a valid one.'

'And if one were to look at it today?'

'The marriage would be a valid one.'

'And if there were any children of that marriage?'

Strougal spread his hands wide.

'They would be legitimate.'

In cross-examination, Warrender came in to the attack.

'This certificate – you say that it is a public document?'

'Yes. It is a note of the performance of a marriage ceremony in a synagogue in Neuberg.'

'Is it – or has it been made – the subject of an Order in Council?'

'I do not understand.'

'I think that you do. A copy, properly authenticated, of an entry in a public register will be evidence not merely of the contents of the register, but also evidence of the facts stated therein. Under the Evidence Act of 1933, an Order in Council can be made with regard to the proof of such registers. Why has none been made in respect of this register?'

'Possibly because it has not been called into question.'

'Or because it is not *capable* of acceptance in this country! An Order in Council would make this document admissible without the necessity of proof by an expert witness. Why was this not done in this case?'

'I cannot answer for the conduct of this case. It was not done.'

'I submit that it was not done because this document is not capable of such proof.'

'I cannot comment.'

'I submit that it is because this document is not an entry from a public register as such.'

'You are wrong. It is a public register.'

Warrender continued to press the point but Strougal refused to be shaken. He was a solid witness. The only time he appeared at all moved, and that he showed only by the raising of an eyebrow, was when there was a sudden disturbance at Centre's side. Stephen Kirk was leaving the courtroom. Mr Justice McIver looked annoyed, but Stephen was on his feet and making for the door with a strangely vacant look in his eyes before anyone could move. Centre was reminded of the evening when the man had left Janet at the Callender Hotel. She had not mentioned his reasons for leaving then, and Centre hadn't raised it with Stephen, since. At the moment it was probably explained by the tenseness of the atmosphere and the strain induced by Warrender's probing.

Nor did Centre see anything of Stephen when the court rose. Mr Justice McIver had promised judgment for tomorrow – Friday morning. Centre rang Stephen's London flat that evening and Stephen answered immediately.

'Are you all right?'

'Of course. Why do you ask?'

'Well, this afternoon...'

Stephen seemed a little vague when Centre explained and obviously thought the matter unimportant, for he brushed it aside.

'What did McIver say?'

'Judgment tomorrow.'

'What are our chances?'

'We'll know tomorrow.'

And the next morning Stephen arrived on time, and so did Vasil Karnowski. John Kirk was not there. Mr Justice McIver sat stiff-backed in his seat and peered over his glasses.

'I would,' he began, 'first state that I am conversant with the time and energy which counsel have devoted to the preparation of their cases, and to the expertise with which they have been backed by the solicitors concerned. It has not been an easy case. The facts posed certain inherent difficulties in themselves...'

Carefully, McIver moved through the facts of the case. He was nothing if not efficient; nothing if not precise. There must be no doubts left at the end; his judgment must be clear.

'The affidavits produced by Mr Karnowski, and by Mr Kirk, emphasize that to their knowledge, and they were in the company of the deceased couple at all material times, no marriage ceremony took place. This is basic to the legitimacy issue, of course, and the question must be asked that if a ceremony was entered into, why was the fact not communicated to the two brothers? This is a point I will return to shortly.

'I turn now to the affidavit of and the evidence given by Mr Penry. It spoke, and he spoke, of the putative father describing Stephen Kirk as a "bastard". I think that we cannot read a great deal into this matter – it can hardly be used in such a way as to suggest that it amounts to the cogent evidence demanded to rebut the presumption of legitimacy... Even so, the case for the defence could have been strongly supported by the production of a birth certificate showing Stephen Kirk to be the acknowledged son of Haren and Magda Karnowski – but no such certificate is forthcoming.'

He paused, and his eagle glance flickered over his glasses towards the parties.

'On the other hand, where there is evidence of search and no marriage certificate can be found, then the law may presume a marriage from the evidence that the persons lived together as man and wife. The presumption of marriage in such a case will prevail unless it is rebutted by evidence to the contrary which appears to be conclusive. I would remind counsel of the words of Lord Lyndhurst in *Morris v Davis: The presumption of law is not lightly to be repelled. It is not to be broken in upon or shaken by the mere balance of probability. The evidence for the purpose of repelling it must be strong, distinct, satisfactory and conclusive.*'

Again, Mr Justice McIver glanced around the courtroom.

'These are clear words. Now the defence has produced a certificate and affidavit to the effect that a marriage was celebrated between the deceased parties in a synagogue in Austria. This certificate cannot be regarded as a marriage certificate. But I would remind parties again of the words of my brother Barnard, in *Russell v Attorney General...*'

Mr Justice McIver turned to his notes and read,

'*Where there is evidence of a ceremony of*

marriage having been followed by cohabitation of the parties, the validity of the marriage will be presumed, in the absence of decisive evidence to the contrary.'

He shuffled the papers aside.

'In applying those words I would say this: in my view the issues must come down simply to two. The two brothers knew of no ceremony; but it would seem there was one. But was that ceremony valid as far as formalities in Austrian law are concerned? Indeed, why were the brothers under the impression all these years that there had been no marriage? It is my understanding of the situation, and there can be no other explanation other than deliberate falsehood on the part of the plaintiff, that the brothers thought there was no marriage because this is what Haren and Magda Karnowski also believed. It is possible that they were aware of the German Marriage Law; it is possible they knew that the marriage was formally invalid. So it was never discussed. Why did they never enter into a civil ceremony? The answer may be in their dislike of the régime, or in the circumstances of their flight to England. We shall never know.'

He paused, and the court was silent.

'So we come to the question of the formal validity of the marriage ceremony. On this must hinge my judgment, though it is true that I am not impressed in other respects by

134

the plaintiff's case. In my view the matter is quite clearly disposed of in this one issue. It is this. I cannot accept the reading of Professsor Hensak; I am impressed by the evidence of Mr Strougal. I will say no more.'

He looked up with finality.

'I find that the marriage celebrated in Neuberg between Haren Karnowski and Magda Schneider was a formally valid marriage and is recognized as such in English law. Stephen Kirk is the issue of that marriage and is the legitimate son of his parents. He is therefore entitled to take the grant of letters of administration to their estate, and the request for revocation of that grant on grounds of error by the plaintiff is accordingly dismissed.'

Stephen was still sitting, half stunned, after McIver had left the courtroom. Centre grinned at him.

'Come on, Stephen, you can celebrate. We've won!'

He seemed to come round only when Stenson joined them happily. Stephen shook his counsel's hand, and then waited while Centre and Stenson indulged in a quick consultation. Karnowski had left, but not before Centre caught the furious glance he had thrown in the direction of Stephen Kirk. A few minutes later Centre followed Stephen out of the courtroom.

He was a few yards behind his client, in the

hall, when he saw the two blue-raincoated men step forward and speak to Stephen. One of them laid a hand on Stephen's arm as though to restrain him. Stephen shook it off, angrily. Centre hurried forward.

'What's going on?' he asked. 'What's happening?'

Stephen turned a distressed face in Centre's direction. But before he could utter a word, the shorter and younger of the two men asked.

'Are you Mr Kirk's solicitor?'

Centre nodded.

'Then I wish to inform you that we are police officers and we are placing your client, Mr Stephen Kirk, under arrest.'

Centre gasped.

'This is ridiculous! What on earth is the charge?'

'The charge,' said the police officer, looking at him levelly, 'is murder.'

CHAPTER III

David Centre stood in the narrow, airless room and stared out through the window. There was a tree down there in the yard and its branches carried a dying foliage that Magda Kirk would never see, for she had died in a fire that had swept through her husband's bedroom. A fire that had been started by her son, Stephen Kirk.

Or so the prosecution was going to say.

Centre could hardly believe what was happening. Only yesterday his client had been deeply involved in trying to prove his legitimacy, and now here he was preparing to defend himself on a charge of murder. Matricide, parricide – forbidding terms for particularly unpleasant crimes. Stephen Kirk was charged with them.

As the door opened behind him Centre turned to see Stephen Kirk entering. He was dressed in blue-grey denim and his face was pale. The lock of hair still flopped stubbornly over his forehead but the rest of his hair glistened with water, combed neatly down. Prison precision.

Centre took a seat across the table from Kirk and looked at him carefully. He essayed a brief smile.

'How are you feeling, Stephen?'

'Still stunned.'

Centre nodded in sympathy.

'I understand. It's been a shock. But it will work out. I ... I really came this morning to see who you want to represent you.'

'I want you, Mr Centre.'

'I'm not sure that you're wise, Stephen. I've not been in practice long. I'm small-time stuff. This is a murder charge – it's out of my league. I'm limited in experience – and let's face it, in ability too. There are firms who specialize in criminal cases: I can put you in touch with them–'

'I want you, Mr Centre.'

'Yes, but–'

'You did a good job for me over the Karnowski case, and I want you to handle this ... this crazy nonsense. You *know* me ... you know I couldn't have done this thing. You can convince them of it .'

'Far better,' argued Centre gently, 'to let a criminal lawyer handle your brief–'

'*Will* you act for me, Mr Centre?'

There was a determined jut to Stephen Kirk's jaw. Centre sighed.

'All right, Stephen, if that's the way you want it.'

'That's the way I want it.'

Centre stared at him for a long moment, thoughtfully. Stephen returned the gaze, waiting with almost childish expectation. It was as though he were holding his breath, waiting for Centre to produce a rabbit out of a legal hat. He showed his disappointment when Centre asked,

'Well, you'd better tell me what happened.'

'Happened?'

'I'll want the complete picture. The prosecution will allege that you went to Kirkley Hall and fired the house. Your parents died in that blaze. First, how do you want to plead?'

'Plead? Not guilty, of course!'

'Fine. Now I want your version of what happened?'

'Version? Nothing happened.'

'Stephen,' said Centre patiently, 'the prosecution will say that you went to Kirkley Hall and–'

'I never went there.'

'When I first met you, you said that you had not been back to Linchester for years before your parents died. That's correct, then?'

'Of course.'

'All right... Now can you state your whereabouts on the night they died?'

'It's a long time ago. I'll have to think.'

Centre nodded, his eyes on Stephen's worried face.

'All right. It's too early yet to say what the police have by way of evidence ... but they must have some reason to link you with the fire.'

'I don't understand it! My parents died months ago … the coroner's verdict was accidental death! How can the police suddenly claim it was murder?'

Centre shrugged.

'It would seem that they were never completely satisfied, and now they have new grounds for supposing… You've no idea what new evidence they might have dredged up?'

'None.'

Stephen's face was expressive of complete bewilderment. Centre hesitated, not sure of what to say. He could not doubt Stephen's distress, and yet the police must have good reason to suppose that Stephen was implicated.

'I think,' he said slowly, 'that it is rather important that you should remember what you were doing that evening. Keep thinking about it. Anyway, I'll try to find out more about the police case before we get to the preliminary hearing, and then maybe we'll come up with positive lines of defence. In the meanwhile, keep thinking… I'll be back to see you on Monday.'

Kirk stood up.

'All right, Mr Centre. I'll try to remember. Er … how's Janet?'

'Worried,' replied Centre. 'I think she'll try to get in to see you soon.'

'I'd be grateful if it could be arranged.'

'I'll try to bring her in with me on Monday.

I'll say goodbye for the moment, Stephen.'

Outside, Centre's first reaction was one of relief to be out of the confining atmosphere of the reception room: the thought made him realize in some degree what Stephen must be feeling. He stopped at the first telephone box he saw and rang Paul Iles's number.

'Iles? David Centre here. You've probably heard the news of Stephen Kirk's arrest. It looks as though we'll be employing you again. Can you come around to my office this afternoon?'

Iles could, and would.

He was brought in by a very subdued Janet. He dropped into the chair that Centre offered him with a frown on his battered features. When Centre outlined to him what had happened an expectant and interested gleam came into his eyes.

'You surprise me, Mr Centre. Stephen Kirk, I would have thought, was not the killing type.'

'If there are such types.'

'There are. Stephen Kirk ... well, he doesn't have the *edge*.'

Centre knew what Iles meant. There was certainly something about Stephen Kirk that wasn't *right*, something that made Centre a little uneasy, but whatever it was, it was not that he gave the impression that he was capable of murder. Perhaps Iles had summarized it well, saying that Stephen lacked the edge.

'Well, anyway, I'm preparing the brief to defend him. I shall go ahead and engage counsel, but though we'll get the prosecution case in detail at the preliminary hearing I want to get as much as I can before then.'

Iles leaned forward and fingered his broken nose thoughtfully.

'You want me to do some ferreting.'

'Just that. The police claim – I've spoken with them – that not only was Stephen in Linchester on the night his parents died, but he also visited Kirkley Hall. Stephen says he didn't return to Linchester until after his parents died. I want you to try to find out on what the police base their claim.'

'Can Stephen state where he was that night?'

'He can't remember.'

'Big help!'

'Two things for you to do, then: check on the prosecution witnesses, if you can, and see if you can find out where Stephen was that night.'

Iles shook his head and twisted his face with a doubtful grimace.

'If he can't give a lead, I don't think I'll turn anything up. Still, I'll get the London office on to it, if you let me have his address in London and so on.'

He was lost in thought for a moment, his rugged face screwed in concentration. At last he asked,

'*Was* he in Linchester that night?'

'You mean,' Centre said quietly, 'is Stephen lying? I don't know.'

Iles stared at him and excitement flickered in his glance.

'You think he may be hiding something.'

'I didn't say that. But there is something … odd. Anyway, anything you can turn up, let me have it. You have more experience of crime than I have, no doubt, and you'll probably come up with some angles that are new to me.'

Iles stood up, grinning.

'When you realize just how many hours I've spent following tired little men keeping assignations with doubtful ladies in seedy, broken-down boarding-houses and hotels, you'll know that the great criminal expert is what I'm not. The idea of the "private eye", Mr Centre, is fictional: believe me, life isn't that exciting.'

'You mean, no broads?' asked Centre.

'It has never,' Iles said solemnly, 'been my luck!'

2

For the rest of the afternoon Centre was forced to put aside thoughts of Stephen's defence; there were other matters demanding his attention. He didn't enjoy working on a Saturday afternoon, and couldn't ask Janet and Charles Blake, nor the new receptionist, Marjorie, to do so, but there were a number of conveyancing contracts to be looked at, as well as a few specifications that Don Chambers had left with him on the occasion of his visit to Centre last week. Centre looked at them with interest – these building specifications sent him back to the old days.

It was seven o'clock before he put aside his papers, stretched and yawned. Time to take a drink, and then get himself a meal. He couldn't face the prospect of returning to the flat and cooking something for himself: 'cooking' was a grandiose term for what he did over the cooker anyway.

He left the car parked in Gordon Street and walked down the main road to the town centre. He went into the Callender Hotel for a drink and dawdled over it. The last occasion he had been here was when he had walked Janet home. He must ask her, some time, what Stephen had given her as a reason for suddenly leaving like that. Rather like the way he had done in court. In the bar that evening, Centre had been talking about the Karnowski case; perhaps Stephen was just not prepared to face up to the kind of strain induced by all that affair. But he had a damn sight more to face up to now.

Centre finished his drink and strolled up the road to the only restaurant in town where he could get a meal that was in any way reasonable. It was eight-fifteen now, the Black Spider was fairly busy and his appetite was sharpened. He ordered a large steak, but had hardly started on the thick sirloin when he was aware of someone standing at his elbow.

'Excuse me – do you mind if I join you?'

The other tables were occupied. Centre looked up and saw a thin, desiccated man in a dark suit, neat shirt with his tie carefully knotted below a prominent Adam's apple. His face was pale, his moustache pared to virtual insignificance and his thinning hair was brushed carefully straight back from his forehead. Centre gestured vaguely.

'By all means. Sit down.'

'Thank you.'

The dark-suited man manoeuvred himself into the seat opposite Centre and was lucky to find an eager waiter at his elbow almost immediately. He placed his order and then glanced sharply across the table.

'I think you must be Mr David Centre.'

Centre looked up in surprise.

'I think *you* must be right. But we haven't met?'

'No. But it's part of my business, knowing people. You have an overdraft, Mr Centre. Of some significance. At my bank.'

Centre smiled.

'I do? *Please* let me pass you the salt.'

The little man facing him accepted the salt quite seriously and went on,

'My name is Brian Nathan. I am the manager of a branch bank here in Linchester where your account is held. We didn't meet when you arrived in Linchester – my deputy arranged the overdraft for you. I authorized it, of course, but naturally we would expect no trouble. It is rarely that one comes across a bankrupt solicitor.'

'Amen to that.'

'How is business, Mr Centre?'

'Picking up well enough for you not to worry about my overdraft, Mr Nathan.'

'Oh, I didn't mean it in that light. I have no real worries on that score. Energetic young solicitors don't rank low in my scale of values – from the point of view of business risks. Builders, now, very risky: more go out of business each year than any other businessmen except electrical and television equipment dealers, it seems to me.'

'I'm thinking of setting up neither sideline.'

Nathan deigned to pucker his lips. It was an apology for a smile that convinced Centre that his bank manager had a serious outlook upon life and one that was dictated by a need to sum up people as security risks in the financial sense. Centre gained the impression that Nathan was a cautious man.

'At least you've chosen stirring times to come to live in Linchester,' remarked Nathan, picking at his halibut.

'I have?'

'Well,' said Nathan, and his glance flickered up to Centre, 'there's the apparent murder of the Kirks... I gather you're defending Stephen Kirk.'

'News travels fast.'

'Bad news does. Sad affair. The Kirks have lived a long time in Linchester. Unlucky family, really, in important things...'

Centre was vaguely surprised, but then assumed that Nathan meant the deaths of Harry and Magda and the arrest of Stephen – they could hardly have been regarded as unlucky before this series of events.

'And of course, on another front, there's the tremendous row that's built up in the planning committee. Quite a furore, I gather.'

'What happened?'

'Oh, it all started some time ago, a long while before you arrived in Linchester so you won't know about it. You must realize that Linchester is in the commuting strip and is beginning to expand at an alarming rate. More people are coming in and house prices are rising. But I need hardly tell you that... The fact is that a development plan was put before the planning committee some three years ago, a plan that included considerable building out on Linchester's west boundary. Out past Sandhill village.'

Nathan dabbed at his lips with his table napkin.

'Sandhill is regarded locally as a beauty spot; I see nothing of value there myself but I know that others regard it highly, and there is also the fact that it is surrounded by open land and good agricultural land. The housing development plan would take over much of this and a strong faction in the planning committee was opposed to it.'

'On what grounds?'

'The usual. Amenity. Open spaces. Green belt. Quality of life. Urban sprawl. High density housing. Communications. Destruction of wild life. County and district responsibilities. Cost. They've fought tooth and nail, and every possible objection has been raised at planning and main committee level.'

'And it all came to a head the other evening?'

'It did.'

'What happened?'

Nathan shook his head.

'I can't quite understand it. A *volte face*, really. This is not uncharacteristic of some councillors, of course, but it is a little ... strange, that some leaders in one group should suddenly seem to capitulate and even vote for the opposing point of view. I cannot mention names, but I will say that I am certainly surprised at the way the vote went.'

'The development plan could yet be thrown out by the council.'

'Ah yes,' Nathan countered swiftly, 'if the council were not split by the same factious elements as appeared in the planning committee. One now wonders – will there be a similar capitulation in full council? Will one decision reflect the other?'

'I see. So you think the Sandhill development might well go through.'

As Don Chambers had said that it would. Curious ... how could Chambers be so positive, before the planning committee had met?

'There is many a slip, of course,' Nathan was continuing, 'but if I were a betting man, my money would be on the developers.'

Centre found the thought a cheering one in a way, in view of his link with Chambers, but he did not divulge his feelings to Nathan. Then, as he looked up to the bank manager he thought for one foolish moment that he had spoken his thoughts. Nathan was sitting rigidly, his fork half way to his mouth, his eyes staring fixedly. But not at Centre: his gaze was concentrated across the restaurant. Involuntarily, Centre twisted in his seat to discover the object of Nathan's attention.

It was a small group of people who had occupied a table beyond the far pillar, somewhat recessed from the rest of the room. It would account for neither Nathan nor Centre noticing them earlier. There were two women and two men. One man Centre recognized.

It was Don Chambers.

Yet it was his companion who drew Centre's attention. The man was slight, his shoulders hunched, his features sallow and lined. His hair was long, and a dirty yellowish-grey in colour. At the moment he was in high good humour but somehow his laughter communicated little real pleasure. It possessed a grating undertone that caused Centre to feel vaguely and inexplicably uncomfortable.

Centre turned back, and observed that Nathan had lowered his eyes and was staring at his plate with strict concentration. But the bank manager was not to escape so easily: as the group, leaving the restaurant, drew level with their table Chambers recognized Centre and whooped noisily, dragging his companions across. Centre was aware of Nathan's twitching hairline and then rose to his feet to confront the grinning, half-intoxicated Chambers.

'Hello, Centre! We made it, boy! Lemme be the first to congratulate us!'

Centre assumed he was alluding to the

planning committee that Nathan had referred to earlier.

'We'll keep congratulations until you get home in one piece,' he said. 'I wouldn't earn my fee next time.'

'Hah! Didn't I tell you, Joey, that he was a good lad? Didn't I tell you? Joe, meet my friend and advocate … hic … David Centre. Centre … meet Joe Acton.'

The man with the yellow-grey hair bowed mockingly from the waist and extended his hand. His handshake was flaccid.

'Delighted to make your acquaintance, Mr Centre.'

'And the girls,' shouted Chambers, 'don't forget the girls!'

Doris and Sally were duly introduced. Centre got the impression that Chambers did not know their surnames. Centre hesitated, then turned to Nathan, but Chambers's companion took the initiative.

'Hello, Nathan. How are you after all this time?'

In spite of his earlier surprise, and his obvious distaste at having to speak to Acton, Nathan had recovered his composure. His tone was cold, but civil enough.

'Good evening, Acton. I was not aware that you had returned to Linchester.'

'You know what they say about bad pennies … especially in banks, eh?'

Nathan grimaced, but made no reply.

151

'Business still looking up?' There was a malicious undertone in Acton's voice and it induced a touch of asperity in Nathan's reply.

'There are fewer problems these days!'

'Let's hope it stays that way, eh? Well, good night, Centre, perhaps we'll meet again.'

Chambers chortled; his face was flushed and he was a little unsteady on his feet as he thumped Centre on the shoulder and staggered away after Acton. The two girls giggled along in their wake.

Sitting down, Centre avoided looking at Nathan, and for a few moments the bank manager seemed incapable of speech, as he dabbed an ineffective fork at the food on his plate. After a long silence he muttered, finally,

'That man ... he's an evil, dangerous man.'

It was not the sort of comment that Centre had expected and it was one to which he could make no reasonable answer. It made little difference; it was as though he were not there, for Nathan suddenly began to speak in a rush of words, as he stared fixedly at his plate, almost talking to himself. His voice was strained.

'A dangerous man, a man to avoid. I was surprised to see him there, and I showed it. Bad; a man like Acton can use a situation like that. He can use so many things to obtain the ascendancy. Seven years, seven

152

years since I last saw him but he hasn't changed, not much. Strange, I would have thought that prison would change a man...'

The neat little moustache twitched and Nathan's mouth pulled sideways in an unpleasant grimace.

'Ten years he got, and he deserved every day of the sentence but he must have got remission. Back here in Linchester. It's too bad. How can he come back – how does he have the nerve to show his face in this town again? But he always had nerve. Look at the way he faced up when the rumours started, look how he still convinced the fools ... look how he even convinced me for a time. He was so plausible...'

Centre twisted uncomfortably in his chair. He was not sure that he wanted to hear Nathan's private thoughts. He pushed his plate aside; the steak had not been a particularly good one anyway. The movement seemed to stir Nathan; he hesitated, then looked up with a sour smile.

'You must excuse me, wandering like that... Old wounds heal slowly.'

'You've had dealings with Acton,' Centre remarked.

Nathan stared at him. His eyes had a sad, drifting look as though he were staring regretfully at past events, seeing what he should have done, what he did not in fact do. Centre saw also in Nathan's face a struggle: the little man was conscious of his professional status, and his ethics, his code of silence, and yet he felt a compulsion to talk, and to explain. The pressure of personality finally triumphed over the inhibition of training, and in a sad, hesitant tone Nathan said:

'He made a fool of me. I see no reason now why I should not admit it. I think that I have lived it down, anyway, and after all, I wasn't the only one who was fooled. There were others ... some who lost a great deal ... some of the unlucky ones...'

He checked at that point. It was as though he was about to say something, but thought better of it. His eyes dwelled reflectively upon Centre for a moment, then he went on.

'It was all rather simple, in a way. Acton was a qualified accountant, working for a Linchester firm. But not even I knew that he floated a company – Western Utilities, Ltd. – and it was my bank that in part financed the early dealings of the company. It had some warehouse accommodation at Grangetown. There were eight directors and all seemed above board, but Action was at the back of it. There was no denying that he possessed business acumen: he made the company work and it could have been a good business. But he wanted quick profits. He got them – by embezzlement.'

'Did he, indeed!'

'That wasn't all the tale.' Now he was launched, and in control of Centre's attention, Brian Nathan seemed to have lost all sense of propriety as far as gossip was concerned. Centre felt a little awkward at drawing the bank manager in this way, but suspected that for some reason Nathan required little drawing: he wanted to get the whole thing off his chest, he wanted to tell the world about the iniquities of this man Acton, whom he obviously regarded as an enemy, and if the world in this context meant only David Centre, what did that matter?

'That wasn't all the tale,' Nathan repeated. 'Acton didn't *work* for Western Utilities. He was employed by ... by another firm and he got into trouble with them for falsification of accounts. As soon as that all came out, it was only a matter of time before police enquiries disclosed the whole sad tale concerning Western Utilities. While Acton's employers were preferring charges against him, the Western Utilities creditors heard the bitter story. They heard how Acton had used the firm for his own ends.'

'How did he do it?'

'I said that there were eight directors: in fact they were Acton's nominees. Two of them held the responsibility for signing cheques. But Acton had an arrangement whereby he kept two separate accounts at the bank – one for the company, and one for himself. He also had an arrangement with the directors that certain cheques coming into Western Utilities were handed over to him for accounting purposes. They must have been crazy, but they did it. And when Acton received these cheques, of course, he paid them into the bank accounts, shall we say ... somewhat indiscriminately. As and when orders were placed with Western Utilities and as payments were made to the company some cheques found their way into his private account. Or at least, one to which he had access.

Nathan's moustache twitched angrily.

'In that account he built up his quick profits. Of course, the other directors should have realized what was going on – indeed, they received short prison terms themselves, for they were held to have connived at the practices, but the truth is that he fooled them. They made little out of it personally. But Acton–'

'Did he make off with a great deal?'

'Enough. Enough to hurt a number of local businessmen.'

'The company was wound up when he was caught?'

'That's right: the creditors started to petition for winding up and froze some of the money in the accounts but Acton must have spent, or salted away, a fair amount. It was lost to his creditors – and there were a lot of them. What was left didn't go very far.'

'And Acton got ten years.'

'And deserved it. But now he's back. I don't like to see him in Linchester again. He brings trouble in his wake. Stay away from him, Mr Centre, have no truck with him. He is a dangerous, slippery, and cunning individual. The fact that he knows his way around the financial world makes him even more troublesome...'

Nathan hunched over the table, refusing coffee. He did not look at Centre but seemed lost in thought: when he left he did not even say goodbye. Centre stared at his black coffee and pondered. If Acton was the vicious character that Nathan made him out to be, Centre hoped that Don Chambers wasn't mixed up with him as far as business was concerned. Still, that was Chambers's affair. David Centre wasn't his nursemaid.

Nevertheless, Acton kept coming back to Centre's mind throughout the weekend. When he got to the office he buttonholed Charles Blake. The young legal executive scratched at his thinning hair.

'Acton? Now wait a minute ... yes, that's right, great fuss in the *Linchester Gazette* six or seven years back. He got put away.'

'Who did he work for?'

'Not a clue. Perhaps Janet can tell you.'

'Joe Acton?' Janet looked up; she had a

pretty frown – it wrinkled her nose and somehow accentuated the clean line of her face. 'Who employed Joe Acton? Er … is it important?'

Centre shook his head.

'No. Doesn't matter. Come on, we've got to get along to see Stephen. Forget it, Janet.'

It was in the car that she suddenly gave a cry of triumph.

'Aha! Of course!'

Centre was startled.

'What's the matter?'

'Joe Acton.'

'You know who employed him?'

'But of course. Do I ever fail?' She smiled in pure pleasure.

'Well?'

'Harry Kirk,' she purred.

3

The Eltham Estate consisted of newly made-up roads, neatly laid out with short green lawns running up to bungalows and houses of three separate designs, staggered in frontage and depth of plot in order to achieve an impression of spaciousness in spite of the relatively high density housing per acre. In general terms Centre approved of the layout; the architect employed by Chambers had done as good a job as possible in the restricted circumstances.

Most of the houses he was now driving past had cars parked outside them; it was after five-thirty and the white-collar workers had returned on the short drive from their offices in Linchester. The far end of the estate showed a tell tale haziness in the air – it would be down there that the bulldozers would be at work.

Centre parked the car at the termination of the made-up road and walked across hard rutted earth to the group of wooden huts in the field. He stopped for a moment to watch a bulldozer at work carving great swathes of soil aside, dry, hard and dusty, and then he walked on towards the huts. A burly man in gumboots came out as he approached and nodded; Centre looked through the window and saw the man he wanted to speak to perched on the edge of the table inside, with a tin mug in his hand.

He went inside.

'Centre! Hello, there. Just in time for a mug of tea.'

'It's a long time since I had a mug of tea sweetened by the taste of construction dust.'

Chambers laughed heartily. He was dressed in an old hacking jacket and corduroy trousers tucked into heavy boots. He looked very much at home.

'You can wax poetic about it, old son, because you're well away from it. Believe

159

me, it's filthy stuff, but I've got to drink it to please old Charlie here.'

Old Charlie was the site watchman, a man in his sixties, whose gnarled features betokened an outdoor building site life. It was what the lucky ones came to in the end, better than retirement. Centre stooped to allow the mongrel dog under the table to lick his hand while Charlie poured the tea.

'They told me I'd find you down here, Mr Chambers. I thought that you might like to see this.'

He handed the paper to Chambers and took the tea from Charlie. Chambers exploded in a great guffaw.

'Ha! Listen to this, Charlie! It's the case I was involved in months back, when a couple of coppers picked me up for being drunk in charge or whatever. The police appealed. This is what the judges said ... where was it, Queen's Bench, no less. They said: *It is not necessary for the proper enforcement of the Road Safety Act 1967 that the words "any person who drives or attempts to drive" should be construed to include a person who had been driving or attempting to drive. In the present case the journey was over and in no real sense could the accused be described as the driver. The Act of 1967 required an arrest before a breathalyser test could lawfully be administered at a police station. It could not be said that the express requirement of the Act was met by the voluntary attendance of the accused at the station so that that was the equivalent of arrest enjoined in the Act. The appeal is accordingly dismissed.* You see, Charlie, we won! And *that* to the police!'

He stabbed a gesture in the air exultingly, then turned a beaming face to Centre.

'I thought it would please you,' Centre said.

'You were damned well right! But you needn't have come out.'

'Glad of the excuse: chance to get out in the fresh air.'

'Want a look around the site?'

'Yes, indeed.'

'Bring your mug with you.'

They tramped around the site, past the excavations and the low walls and Chambers pointed out the building lines with a stubby forefinger.

'You're building the flats down there?' Centre asked with interest.

'Right! Good design, eh? Experimental, of course. But if they go we'll shove some up on the Sandhill site.'

'I had a look at the contracts for those flats, as you asked me.'

'Good – hell, that 'dozer makes a noise, don't it!'

Centre raised his voice.

'I also took a look at the specifications – not strictly my business, but I'd advise *you* to have another look at them.'

'Why so?' bellowed Chambers as the bull-dozer trundled past and the dust drifted over in a great cloud.

'You'll be in trouble if you don't,' Centre said, coughing. 'They'll be Purpose Group III buildings and you can have combustible materials in the separating walls only if the buildings separated are not single storey and more than 30,000 square feet floor area, or are not multi-storey buildings, compart-mented. Your specifications don't comply.'

'Bloody hell! You sure?'

'You check. And take a look at your floor load allowances too. The general minimum imposed floor load is 30 pounds per square foot over the whole floor area. With your designs I reckon you're overloading.'

Chambers spat out a mouth full of dust and glared after the retreating bulldozer.

'Anything else?'

'Minor points,' yelled Centre. 'Your thermal insulation – be cheaper to use boarding nailed to battens ... float them on a layer of glass fibre. Drape the layer over wooden joists, and have a lath and plaster ceiling about three-quarters of an inch thick.'

'Pugging?'

'On the ceiling, of a weight of not less than 17 pounds per square foot.'

'Hell's bells, Centre, why don't you come

work for me?' shouted Chambers, red in the face, the dust darkening his fair hair.

'Because I've got a job. I shouldn't really poke my nose in like this anyway; it's none of my business.'

'Well, keep making it your business – as long as you don't charge me for the advice! By the way, I gather you've got a murder case on your hands now.'

Centre nodded.

'Stephen Kirk.'

'Well, I can't blame him.'

For a moment, the statement did not register with Centre, then he glanced curiously at Chambers. The man's broad face suddenly flushed and Centre obtained the impression that Chambers wished he had not spoken.

'What do you mean?' Centre asked.

'Mean? Nothing!'

'You said that you couldn't blame Stephen Kirk. For what?'

Chambers looked unhappy.

'Well ... I didn't mean it that way. I meant that ... well, if he did knock off Harry Kirk, well...'

Centre's mouth was grim.

'Well what?'

Don Chambers was all at once no longer a successful businessman: he was like a small boy caught with his fingers in the jam. He looked around, almost wildly, as though for some distraction that would save him. There was none, and Centre was insistent.

'Aw hell, all I'm trying to say is that if Stephen Kirk did knock off his old man, well, Harry Kirk deserved it!'

'Why?'

Centre's question came like a whipcrack. The bulldozer had stopped work. The field was very silent. And Chambers had changed yet again. His mouth had tightened and his head seemed to have settled pugnaciously into his shoulders. There was a hardness in the line of his jaw and a new hardness in his eyes too, a calculating look that Centre had not seen in the man before. He suddenly realized how imperfectly he knew Don Chambers, and with it came the realization that Chambers could be a stubborn man ... and more: he could be a dangerous man, and a vicious enemy. In addition, Centre obtained the overall impression that this was how Chambers had looked upon Harry Kirk – as an enemy.

'I'm sorry, Centre. I've nothing more to say. Let's leave it at that.'

Centre had the sense to do as Chambers suggested.

The builder had regained his good humour by the time they got back to the hut and pressed Centre for more details concerning the specifications. Centre was unable to get away until well after seven and when he did he drove through the estate until he found a telephone kiosk. He left the Aston Martin, and rang Paul Iles's private number.

'Iles? Centre here. I'm sorry to bother you but can you spare me a few minutes this evening? I'd like a word.'

'Of course, why not? You want to call here? You eaten yet? Why not drive around and we'll have a bachelors' fry-up together, with a couple of cans of beer.'

It sounded a good idea, and Centre said so.

Iles lived out at Sault Hill, in a small bungalow with lead-paned windows, a concrete drive and no garden worth discussion. There was a small Renault parked in the drive and Centre pulled the Aston Martin in behind it. He suddenly felt that his car was pretentious.

Paul Iles didn't think so.

'I admire that,' he said, walking around it and whistling between his teeth. 'Me, I can't afford one, and whoever heard of an enquiry agent doing a bit of investigating in an Aston Martin anyway? Come inside and have a beer.'

It was welcome. The dust from the field had dried Centre's throat and he downed the beer almost too quickly to be polite. Iles grinned, and gave him a refill.

'Five minutes and the mixed grill will be up. Cafeteria service, I'm afraid.'

Egg, sausages, steak, mushrooms and to-matoes and Centre was hungrier than he had realized. He squinted up at Iles, sitting massively across the table from him in a thin blue sweater.'

'You're in the wrong business.'

'My old man ran a restaurant. Still does, as a matter of fact. Try it some time.'

'I will. Not leanings that way yourself?'

'Not really. The old man wanted me to come in, but I got spoiled. Playing rugby for a London club, and a League scout from Huddersfield grabbed me. I signed on and three years later came out with a bit of capital, and a somewhat battered face. This one—' he fingered his nose, – 'was one of my own lads. He tried to plant one on a forward on the other side. In the scrum, you know. Just grazed the other bloke, but laid me out, clean as a whistle, with the follow through. That was me finished – if they were going to affect me manly beauty I was no longer interested.'

'And then?'

Iles shrugged.

'Drifted a bit. Didn't really want to go back to the Smoke. Tried a commercial travelling job and then one night got caught in a fracas outside the hotel. Two layabouts giving this middle-aged bloke a going-over. I persuaded them it was ungentlemanly. I got quite excited, then, when I realized the chap being worked over was employed as an enquiry agent. Next thing I knew, I was in the Carlsen agency.'

'Just like that.'

'They were impressed by my references,' said Iles with a grin. Centre smiled back, noting Iles's shoulders again, and his battered face. He knew what he meant.

'More beer?'

Iles crossed to the refrigerator and Centre stared out of the window at the back garden, a small piece of turf, triangular in shape. The grass was long.

'No time to cut it,' said Iles defensively. 'I rent this place, of course, and the firm meet me halfway with it. They also rent a room for me in town, in the Halstead building ... not that I'm ever there, it seems to me. Anyway, enough of this. What's on your mind?'

'I went to see Stephen Kirk this morning. He still says he can't remember what he was doing that night ... he thinks he went to the cinema.'

Iles groaned.

'That doesn't help much. I've not yet got the London office to turn anything up.'

'Well, keep trying. Now I've also asked you to check on the police witnesses – find out what sort of evidence they'll be producing at the preliminary hearing.'

'Ahuh!'

'Well, I'm now asking you to widen your scope a bit. I want you to find out all you can about Harry Kirk.'

'The deceased gentleman?'

'None other. It seems to me that if it was murder, and my client is innocent, it will be of considerable help to us to discover the sort of man Kirk was, to find out if he had any enemies. And while you get on with that, I'm going to have a crack at Stephen – he's told me nothing yet about the causes of his quarrel with his father. I think it's time I knew all about it. Moreover–'

He broke off.

'What's the matter?' he asked.

Paul Iles was smiling; it broadened his face, lined it, and drew attention away from his scarred nose.

'Why are you smiling?'

'I was just thinking. Put you next to an enquiry agent and you get bitten by the bug. Happened to me, and it seems to happen to you too.'

'I'm just thinking of the best way to defend my client,' replied Centre, a little ruffled, but smiling in spite of himself. 'If we can point to enemies, and possible guilt elsewhere, it's another way of defending him.'

'Agreed.' The twinkle remained in Iles's eye. 'You were about to say?'

Centre hesitated.

'Well, the reason why I ask you to look into Harry Kirk's background is that it has just come home to me this afternoon that he might well have enemies. So we need to know all we can about him and his background.'

'You'd already said that. You were about to say something else.'

Centre still hesitated. It was like the betrayal of a friendship. But at last he said it.

'I spent the last few hours with another client of mine. Don Chambers. He – he said something disturbing. Or perhaps it wasn't so much what he said, as the way he said it. He knew Harry Kirk. He didn't like him.'

He looked squarely at Iles.

'I want to know whether Chambers disliked Harry Kirk enough to kill him.'

4

'You would not, of course, be presuming upon an old friendship?'

'Oh, hardly that, George. But it is whisky and soda, isn't it?'

'It is indeed. I shall now wait, after you've bought the drinks, to see if you take out your little notebook and put the entry down under expenses. Then I shall know.'

'You've an evil, suspicious mind, George. Just because I want to buy you a drink, you think I'm trying to pump you.'

'Like hell you're trying to pump me. If you had the chance you'd even flush me out with an enema.'

George Denton settled back on the padded seat in the lounge and watched Paul Iles buy the drinks. He liked Iles, though normally he would have no truck with enquiry agents, for they were a slimy, dangerous breed, in his view. But Paul Iles was different: to start with, you could trust him, and there was the added point that he could also be relied upon to play fair with his sources of information. If there was a story in it, Iles would see to it that it went to the right man, just as long as the interests of his clients and his agency were protected. In other words, there was a mutual trust between the two of them, both were aware of it, both stuck to it. Yes, George Denton liked Paul Iles and didn't mind in the slightest that he was about to be pumped.

'Cheers, George.'

'You've got a throat like an ostrich,' remarked Denton with a growl, as he sipped his whisky. 'How the hell you can drown your insides with that evil-smelling bitter I can't understand.'

'When I reach your age, George, maybe I'll have cultivated your sophisticated tastes.'

'I hope the fifteen years' difference also sharpens your wit. But there, I suppose I need a dull stone on which to sharpen my own.'

'Well, I agree it's blunt enough to require an occasional whetting. Anyway, enough of the banter. How's business?'

'The opening shot in the interrogation. Don't prevaricate, young Iles. Get down to it. What do you want to know?'

'You distress me, George! Why must you be so directly *professional* about these things? Naked competence, I call it!'

'Call it what you will.' Denton's tone was urbane. 'But get the questions out of the way and then maybe we can have a social evening.'

Iles grinned and held up a huge hand in token surrender.

'All right. I'm aware that your social standing as editor of the *Linchester Gazette* demands that you are dragged out from under the table each night. We'll get down to questions first, and serious drinking later. All right, George, I want to know about Harry Kirk.'

'Do you, indeed?'

'Indeed, I do.'

'What, precisely?'

'Precisely, everything.'

'Tall order.'

'You should know.'

Denton chewed at his pendulous lower lip thoughtfully. It was perfectly obvious that

Paul Iles had been retained by young Centre, the solicitor defending Stephen Kirk. It was equally obvious that in assisting Paul Iles now, there could be an early story when the time came, before the big agencies stepped in. If there was a story other than the obvious one, that is ... the obvious one being that the police were absolutely right, and were already holding the killer of Harry and Magda Kirk. Magda Kirk ... nice woman, he remembered meeting her a couple of times. Quiet; unassuming; reliable. Qualities not present in her husband.

'Harry Kirk,' he said thoughtfully. 'Lived here a long time, you know. Lot can happen in well over twenty years.'

'Salient points, George. You're a newspaperman. You've got a nose. You know, instinctively, what is and what isn't important. I want the important stuff ... on Harry Kirk.'

Denton's little eyes squinted into Paul Iles's battered, cheerful face.

'I'll do my best,' he said, and paused, thinking. Nearer thirty years, than twenty.

'Harry Kirk came to Linchester in the 1940s, as I remember, with his wife, son and cousin. It was quite obvious that he intended fitting in, so to speak, because although none of them had much English they really worked at it. A motivated family, you might say, in many ways.'

Denton pulled out a pipe and lit it rumi-

172

natively. Iles waited, and sipped his beer.

'It was quite remarkable the way Kirk got on. He had nothing – if you count personal charm and the ability to influence people for nothing. No money is what I meant, of course. That soon changed. Within eight years he had two factories in Linchester and Grangetown, and his cousin shortly qualified as a solicitor and moved to Linthorpe.'

'How was the family regarded in Linchester?'

'You'll not hear anything against Magda Kirk; a fine woman. But Harry ... well, I don't know what it was. Maybe it was his eagerness to get, well, assimilated, maybe it was his success in business, maybe it was his buying Kirkley Hall, maybe it was the flamboyance of the man, his overt charm ... hell, you name it. He just wasn't popular, you know? Could be jealousy, of course, but few people seemed to like him.'

'Liking is one thing. Dislike, of the sort strong enough to lead to violence, is another.'

'I agree. I could give you a list of five or six people who hated Harry Kirk's entrails, but most of them would neither have the guts nor the intelligence to think of knocking him off. The others, well, I guess they'll have sublimated the urge in other directions anyway.'

'But did he have any *real* enemies?'

Denton sucked on his pipe thoughtfully.

'You name me a businessman who doesn't. With Harry Kirk, well… You know, Iles, in my experience enemies arise out of two situations, basically: work and sex. Ask a man who his enemies are and he'll tell you that he's made them in the course of his business life or his sex life. Harry Kirk was no exception.'

'I think you're oversimplifying generally, but it applies to Harry Kirk?'

'I think so. Let's take his work first. I think, for instance, that you should look into his business interests. I think you should look into the prosecution he brought seven years ago–'

Denton caught the gleam in Iles's eye, and remarked in an interested tone, 'I gather you're already looking into that.'

Iles shrugged noncommittally and Denton went on,

'You should look also at a man called Lawson, an employee of his, who has, or thinks he has, little reason to love the family.'

'What about the family itself?'

Denton shrugged.

'Well, Harry and Magda got on, I think, because she was prepared to put up with the man she had. Let's put it straight: Harry Kirk had immense charm but he was hard as a businessman should be. Maybe his private life got a bit mucky, but well, that sort of thing happens. His cousin remained in close touch, I think – John Kirk, that is – I think they had common business interests and I understand that John Kirk handled Magda's affairs. The other cousin, Karnowski, well I didn't even know he existed until the recent case.'

Iles finished his drink and sat staring with narrowed eyes at his empty glass.

'What about Don Chambers?' he asked abruptly.

Denton raised his grey eyebrows.

'You mean would he have any reason to … now then, that's a thought. Are you saying–?'

'I'm not saying anything.'

'Oh, you know me, Paul, I'd never quote you. Misquote you, yes, but quote you, never. Don Chambers, eh…? Yes, indeed!'

Iles looked up; Denton's old eyes were glittering.

'Tell me,' demanded Iles.

'It's an angle I hadn't thought too much about,' said Denton with an air of surprise at his own lack of perspicacity. 'You see, Harry Kirk infiltrated into Linchester society and the Linchester business world, as good as eradicated his accent and then in a determined effort to outdo the residents turned to good works. He became a councillor – by dint, some would say, of providing plenty of ale for his workers!'

'Don't tell me such mediaeval tricks still

work in Linchester!'

'Don't interrupt. Fact is, he became a councillor, a member of the planning committee and, for the last three years, chairman of the planning committee.'

'So?'

'He exercised a great deal of influence on that committee. A great deal. Now about three years ago who should come along but a certain gentleman with a development plan for Sandhill Down. It just so happens, of course, that Kirkley Hall lies out past Sandhill, but I've no doubt that Harry Kirk's motives in fighting that development plan were dictated by altruism alone. Councillors are above suspicion.'

'You are hinting, George, but not stating.'

'Then state I will. I hadn't indulged in any cerebration on this theme before, but don't you see? For three years the Sandhill development scheme has been blocked. Blocker-in-chief, Harry Kirk, as chairman of the planning committee. Suddenly, friend Harry dies and what happens? Planning committee suddenly, and surprisingly, pass the scheme. Gainer-in-chief? One could say, a certain Mr Chambers.'

Iles was silent for a moment.

'I can hardly believe that a man would ... remove another for the sake of a few houses.'

'Few houses?' Denton laughed. 'You want

to take a look at that scheme, my friend. You do indeed.'

'I'll get another drink, George.'

'On me, old boy.'

'Nuts.'

At the bar Iles's mind was churning over. Centre had said that Chambers had obviously disliked Harry Kirk strongly. Now Harry Kirk was dead, it was true that Chambers stood to gain ... but what? How much? Maybe Centre himself would know: he had dealings with Chambers anyway.

Iles took the drinks back to the table and sat there silently. George Denton puffed at his pipe, his keen old eyes watching a group of people that had just come in, laughing noisily, and leaning against the bar of the cocktail lounge. Iles looked up.

'You did say, George, that for Harry Kirk enemies could come out of his business life, or his sex life.'

'I did, and you could not reintroduce the topic at a more convenient time.'

'How do you mean?'

George Denton smiled knowingly and tapped his pipe out into the ashtray.

'Well, Harry Kirk had a good wife, but perhaps she didn't like the social life as he did, or perhaps he was bored, or perhaps he was just a womanizer. No matter. Let's just say that he had his fling.'

'And?'

'If you look over your shoulder, towards the bar you'll see a lady.'

'The blonde?'

'That's right.'

Denton sucked at his empty pipe.

'Haven't you heard about her?'

5

Stephen Kirk's face lit up when he saw that Janet had accompanied Centre to visit him. His eyes were animated and he walked forward to take both her hands, greeting her with an effusiveness that seemed to embarrass her a little. She glanced almost apologetically towards Centre, but he looked away; he thought that he ought to give Stephen a moment with her, but she seemed to decide otherwise because she sat down beside Centre. Stephen took the seat facing them.

He smiled at Janet.

'I'm more than pleased you came.'

'You're looking well, anyway,' she said.

He wasn't. His face was pale with the strain of his confinement and he had obviously slept badly. His appearance was neat enough with his denims carefully buttoned and his hair brushed back, apart from the inevitable errant lock on his forehead, but his eyes were shadowed and he had difficulty in keeping his hands still.

'Any further developments?'

'Not really,' replied Centre. 'I've engaged an enquiry agent to dig around, but what I really want to do is ask you whether you've remembered yet what you were doing the night your parents died.'

'The police put me through all this when they questioned me–'

'And you gave them no answer then and you've given me no answer since.'

'I think I went to see a film, a Russian film, in one of the Academies–'

'Are you being honest with me, Stephen?'

Centre was aware of Janet's head turning in his direction but he went on.

'You've got to remember that most of what you say can be checked. Now I'm acting for you, not against you, and if I'm to do that effectively I must have your confidence. When you lie to me, you must lie for a reason. Do you have reason to lie, Stephen?'

'I haven't lied.'

Centre doggedly ignored the involuntary angry gesture that Janet made in support of Stephen's outburst.

'Maybe not, but I'm being perfectly clear, I trust, when I say that you are being singularly unhelpful in the preparation of your own defence. All I have had from you till now is an assertion that you cannot remember where you were that night and an insistence that

179

wherever you were, you were not in Linchester. Now is that the truth, to start with?'

'Yes. Of course it is!'

Centre observed him in silence for a moment. Janet was quiet also but there was anger in the way she held her head.

'All right. What happened seven years ago?'

'What?'

'Why did Harry Kirk throw you out?'

Stephen opened his mouth, and shut it again. Janet tried to save him.

'I don't see what that has to do with a murder trial!'

'And *I* don't see,' replied Centre,' what this has to do with you, Miss Sanders. You're here to take notes, if I wish notes to be taken, not to make observations.'

Janet controlled herself with an effort but her eyes held his and plainly told him what she thought of him. Stephen shook slightly, and his tongue flickered in the corner of his mouth.

'I agree with Janet. What's it got to do with–'

'I'll tell you what it's got to do with this. When your name is dragged into court they'll be saying that you murdered your father and your mother. They'll say that you did it, they'll say how you did it, and they'll say why you did it. They'll add strength to the case they present by showing that relations between yourself and your father have been bad for years. They'll say, they'll insinuate, they'll prove, I don't know what they'll do, but they will hammer home the fact of the estrangement and I'm bloody sure that the way things are going they'll know what they are talking about and I won't. And I'm supposed to be defending you. Now, will you tell me what happened seven years ago?'

Stephen's head fell forward on to his hands.

'Pull yourself together,' Centre said brutally, 'and let me have the truth.'

Janet rose suddenly and marched across to the window. She stared out, her arms folded across her breast, her back stiff with indignation. Centre glanced in her direction: he had no doubt he'd pay for this on the return journey to the office. But when he looked back Stephen began to talk. His voice was strained.

'When ... when I was sixteen Dad got me to leave school. I wasn't keen to stay anyway, but I wasn't keen to do what he wanted either. He wanted me to train as an accountant, and I suppose he was right. No, dammit, he *was* right, I know that now, but I kicked against it at the time. I wanted to turn to law like Cousin John but Dad insisted. He said it was the sort of training that would gear me up properly to take over the business interests that he was building up.'

He hesitated.

'In those days he was building the business for me. He said so.'

There was a defiant note in his voice. Centre nodded.

'Did your father have some regard for you in those days?'

'I think so, yes. He had plans... Anyway, I went into the firm at Linchester first, and Dad made me work in the costing section. Then he moved me from department to department during the next three years. I started working for accountancy exams. – evening classes at Linchester Tech. I got Part I of the ACCA.'

'And then?'

'Then, after a while, Dad had me moved to Grangetown. He'd decided to centralize accounts there and he put me to work with his chief account. He was called–'

'Acton. Yes, I've met him.'

Janet had turned back from the window; she was listening in spite of herself.

'Well,' Stephen continued, 'I didn't know what was happening, it's the honest truth. I was working under Acton, and I did what I was told. It's true that I checked a number of his transactions, and I worked with him on a number of sales returns and internal audits during the next two years, but I saw nothing wrong. I wasn't experienced enough to see it, that was the trouble. And he was in charge – I just did what I was told.'

'And what was going on?'

'The technical terms,' Stephen said bitterly, 'are "kiting" and "lapping". Money is transferred between two accounts, recording the receipt prior to the balancing date and the payment after the balancing date. That's "kiting". The other trick is to hold up part of amounts received and "lap" them with subsequent receipts. You can do that indefinitely, in order to make the record of receipts equal to the amount banked.'

'But these are, well, petty frauds surely – and short term?'

'Not the way Acton played it. Besides, they were only part of his system. He ran a special account of his own and paid into it cheques on which he'd forged signatures – he then charged them to credit balances on customer accounts. I could go on and on – every trick in the book, and he was swinging it.'

'I still don't see–'

'It was all part of a bigger thing. He'd floated another company, as you probably know–'

'Western Utilities Ltd.'

'That's right. Much of the cash which he

creamed off from Dad he used in the short term to finance his company. At the beginning at least.'

'And you got caught up in the whole thing.'

Stephen nodded. He was silent for a while. Centre did not look at Janet, who had moved away from the window now.

'Dad played hell,' Stephen said at last. 'He got me up in the office and he blew his top. He blamed me as much as Acton; said I should have sorted it out, seen what was happening, protected the family firm. I lost my temper in the end, even called him names, Polish redneck, things like that. He went absolutely spare. It went on for days … and then, incredibly it seemed to me, he said that he was going to prefer charges against me, too. It was then that I hit him.'

His lips tightened.

'He never forgave me for that blow.'

The room was silent, and only their minds echoed to that distant quarrel. Centre stared at Stephen's lowered head. What had the sadness in his voice signified? Regret for the quarrel? Regret for the lack of reconciliation? Regret for his mother who had played no part in it and yet had suffered the break with her son? He had to ask the next question.

'And you never came back to Linchester. Until after they were dead?'

Again Centre was conscious of Janet at his elbow.

'I ... I never came back. Dad didn't press charges in the end, but on condition I left. I went to London. I never came back.'

Centre nodded slowly.

'All right. That's about all for now. I'll be in again tomorrow. Keep you up to date with developments, if there are any. There's nothing else you want to tell me?'

'There's nothing to tell.'

'Did you know Acton was out now ... and in Linchester?'

Stephen's eyes were puzzled.

'No. I didn't know that.'

Janet waited behind to talk to Stephen for a moment before she joined Centre in the corridor. They did not speak as they walked out of the building into the sunshine. He opened the door of the Aston Martin and she got in without a word. He slipped into the driving seat.

'I was afraid,' he said, 'that you'd go off on public transport and in high dudgeon.'

She was unamused, and obviously did not trust herself to speak for a moment. Then she said with some bitterness,

'You behaved towards Stephen in a quite unnecessarily brutal fashion. You are supposed to be defending him, and yet you treated him as though you were the prosecutor and believed him guilty of this

185

appalling crime!'

Centre drove the car carefully out of the car park.

'I decided he needed rough handling.'

'Godlike,' she said, scoffing. 'He sits there and pronounces – he needed rough handling. Well, you handled him with the gloves off, all right.'

'I got what I wanted.'

'And what was that?'

'My behaviour was calculated and deliberate. I acted that way not because that's *me*, but because I had an end in view. I wanted to see whether he could take rough handling ... it could be important in a cross-examination situation. Secondly, I wanted to bring home to him that half-truths are dangerous, that he must hide nothing from me, and I also wanted the full story of the Acton affair.'

'Well, you got it.'

'Maybe so. But there's more to this, even yet. Don't you feel that there's something about Stephen that's ... well, not *right?*'

Janet shrugged.

'He seems preoccupied at times, I admit but–'

'It's more than that. It's almost as though he doesn't *care,* sometimes. That was another reason for trying to shock him out of things.'

'I still don't understand.'

'Well, take the night he ditched you at the Callender, and I had to take you home.'

He realized that the word 'had' was somewhat ill-chosen.

'He explained that,' Janet said. 'He felt ill, and thought he'd better get back home.'

'Maybe so, and perhaps it was true. But you know him better than I. Is he a liar, Janet?'

'What on earth do you mean?'

'You know what I mean, Janet. You know as well as I; you can see it in his face, you can see it in his eyes, pick it up in his hesitation, in the inflection in his voice!'

She remained stubbornly silent.

'Dammit, girl, can't you see it? When I asked him, at the end, when I asked him if he had come back to Linchester at all before their death, he was lying, Janet, he was lying. *I'm certain of it!*'

CHAPTER IV

The trouble with being a solicitor was that one couldn't pick one's clients. There were many things about the law and the legal profession that appealed to David Centre: the majesty of the law, its intricacies, its precision, its logicality and its illogicality, the hidden barbs that lay in wait for the unwitting litigant, the traps, the quirks, the quillets... And he liked the fact that it enabled him to meet people and to help and advise them – what man did not like advising another? He enjoyed assisting people to obtain justice, or compensation, or redress.

But there was also the other aspect.

There was the fact that much of the work that came into an office was dull, drudgery, dry as the proverbial dust. Worse than that, however, was the type of situation where he was called upon to advise particularly unfortunate people, advise them that the law could not assist them, tell them that they had no hope of obtaining justice, point out to them the occasional yawning gap that lay between law and justice. There was the deserted wife, the occasional child torn between bickering parents, there was the

eternal parade of pomposity and un-
pleasantness.

This was one of those days. He was visited
by two individuals for whom he could feel
no pity and yet towards whom he could not
suppress a savage, righteous anger. It was
wrong to castigate on moral grounds for
these were sick; it was wrong to judge but he
was incapable of resisting judgment. The
one case involved a man of sixty with a
record of offences involving indecent expo-
sure, and he was now fearing a charge of
attempted rape upon a nine-year-old child.
The other was concerned with suspected
incest.

It was curious that two such cases should
come to him in one morning when they were
of the kind that he might go for months or
even years without touching; two cases involving sexual offences, two cases suggesting
aberrations which involved him emotionally.
The old man came tremulously, awaiting
arrest but wanting to see a solicitor first,
before the police reached him; the other
came, virago-like, hauling in triumph a terri-
fied sixteen-year-old daughter with arms like
sticks, triumphant in her accurate reading of
her husband's character and her daughter's
mental retardation. She seemed almost
disappointed when Centre told her that the
permission of the Director of Public Prose-
cutions would be necessary before a

prosecution could be brought and that she should go to the police anyway. Her disappointment seemed to be due to the fact that she might not be proved right, publicly – her daughter's welfare counted for nothing.

The interviews soured the morning for him. He could not clear his mind of the sad picture of society that they presented and it was with a feeling that could be described only as yearning that his mind drifted to Canada, to remember the clean, glacier-sheathed line of Mount Victoria, and the jagged ramparts of the Queen Elizabeth Ranges mirrored in an icy, green-blue lake.

He felt he wanted company, wanted to talk to someone and he walked across the corridor to the room where Janet worked. Her chair was empty: he saw the shadow of her form through the glass door leading into Charles Blake's room. He hesitated for a moment and even contemplated walking through to reception to speak, about nothing, to the new girl, Marjorie, but the thought of her long, shoulder-length hair, over-made-up eyes, and vacuous gaze deterred him. Disconsolately, he reached over to look at the book lying on Janet's desk. Its title surprised him: 'Parry – *The Law of Succession*.

He hadn't realized that Janet had taken to reading law. She came in through the door-way as the thought crossed his mind and he repeated the thought aloud to her.

'Law books?' She looked puzzled. 'Oh, that! It's not mine. It belongs to Charles – he must have left it on my desk. I gather he's taking some examination or other.'

Blake, hearing Centre's voice, appeared in the doorway.

'What examinations, Charles?' Centre asked him lifting the book in one hand. Blake shrugged a little shamefacedly.

'Well, thing is, Mr Centre, you know I was mainly a litigation clerk with my last firm and now I'm doing a wider range of stuff so I thought I might as well mug up on some law and take the necessary three papers for the Fellowship examination of the Institute of Legal Executives.'

Centre smiled.

'Good idea. Let me know if there's anything I can do to help at any time. Which papers will you do?'

'I thought the two Conveyancing papers, and Probate and Succession.'

'Hence *Parry*.'

'That's right.'

A silence fell. Janet and Blake stood there dumbly and Centre suddenly felt embarrassed, without knowing why. Perhaps it was due to the fact that Janet seemed not to have forgiven him for his attitude towards Stephen Kirk. On the way back in the car he had said to her,

'Don't misunderstand me, Janet. I'm sure

he's lying when he said he'd not been back to Linchester. I feel it intuitively.'

She had been decidedly cool.

'It is impossible, Mr Centre, to believe anything that anyone says, at any time – unless you act on experience and trust. No one person knows what another thinks, or why he acts or says what he does. You have to fall back on trust in the end. I could say that there have been times recently when I too have felt that there was something odd about Stephen, when I've felt there was something strange in his behaviour and his mannerisms. But that's a different thing from saying that he's a deliberate liar, a fraud, and … and a murderer.'

But that, Centre knew, was no answer.

It still lay there between them today, nevertheless; a slight strain in their relationship. He stuck his hands in his pockets.

'I've got a bit of a headache,' he said. 'I'm going out for a while, to get some fresh air. I don't think I have any further appointments this morning, do I, Janet?'

She shook her head.

He left the office and walked down towards the Town Hall. He passed the offices used by the other firms in Linchester and looked up to their windows, and the gilt lettering gleaming in the morning sunlight: *Solicitors and Notaries Public*. He read off the names to himself – *Gill, Scarfe and Doncaster;*

Guest, Redman and Turner; why were these and all the others always in threes? Magical number. Seven was too many. Disconsolately he walked into the square. If he had only been ten years old he'd have found a tin to kick.

He stood at the pavement edge, waiting for the lights to change so that he could cross the road, and someone touched his arm.

'Hello, Centre. Well met.'

Centre stared at the speaker foolishly. He was aware that he should know him but was yet unable to fix a name. Gradually the features registered: the sallow face squinting up into his, the deep lines around the eyes, the long, yellowish-grey hair.

'Oh … Acton, isn't it?'

Joe Acton nodded, and smiled. His teeth were grey-filmed and one canine was missing. His tongue flickered in the gap.

'I trust that things are well with you?'

'Well enough,' admitted Centre, as they crossed the road together, threading their way through an opposing tide of basket-armed women.

'How's your client bearing up?'

'Stephen Kirk? He's bearing up,' replied Centre non-committally. Acton was undeterred.

'You seen Don recently?'

'Chambers? Well, I saw him out at the site

a couple of days ago.'

'That'll be the Eltham site.' Acton bared his teeth in a wolfish grimace. 'Did he talk about the Sandhill deal at all?'

The hunched shoulders bumped into Centre as they walked and the solicitor was unable to suppress the involuntary shudder of distaste that affected him. There was something about Acton that set his nerves on edge.

'No. I meant to have a word with him about it, but we got involved with other matters and just never got around to it.'

'Well, I suppose he couldn't have told you about recent developments anyway: after all, it was only last night.'

'What happened last night?'

Acton showed considerable satisfaction.

'The full council not only approved the planning committee recommendations, but have decided that tendering further will be unnecessary, in view of previous applications made and the excellence of Don's plans.'

'That's unusual ... won't other local firms object?'

'I doubt it. I gather Don will be using some of them anyway, to some extent. Sub-contracting, you know.'

'Will he, indeed?'

They paused at the next corner, Centre intimating that he was proceeding in a direction different from Acton's.

'Yes,' said Acton. 'After all, it's a big project. You know how big. It'll need a company, of course, to run it. Don will be forming one, once the finance comes through. And it will.'

'He expressed some doubt previously–'

'It'll come through. And when it does, he'll be asking you to set up the company. I gather,' added Acton, 'he'll also be putting you on a retainer to act as legal adviser. He seems to be somewhat taken with you, Centre.'

With a brief wave of his hand the man went on his way. Centre stared after him for a moment, then thoughtfully turned back towards Gordon Street. What had the bank manager – Brian Nathan – said about Acton? An evil and dangerous man, he'd said. He'd warned Centre to have nothing to do with him. A man convicted of fraudulent conversion, embezzlement, and the Lord knew what else. When he got back to the office he hesitated for a long while before he picked up the telephone.

At last he rang Don Chambers.

'Ah, Centre! What can I do for you?'

Centre found difficulty in getting to the point.

'Well, nothing really. I … I just heard this morning that the full council–'

'Ah, you heard the good news. They've passed the planning committee recommendation, and they're giving me the go-ahead. No wonder you rang – thinking of all that conveyancing lolly, eh?'

'Not exactly,' replied Centre carefully. 'It's just that the information was given to me by Mr Acton.'

There was a brief silence; when Chambers spoke, it was non-committally.

'Ahuh. So?'

'So it just occurred to me that he knew rather a lot about your affairs.'

'That's not surprising. He's involved in them.'

'I don't follow.'

Don Chambers's voice had cooled even further.

'I shall be asking you to form a company for me, Centre, to run the Sandhill development. I'll give you a list of subscribers and all that jazz. Joe Acton will be one of them.'

'Acton will be one of the directors of your company?'

'That's right. And you'll be retained as legal adviser.'

Centre ignored the last remark.

'You know what you're doing, I suppose. You know Acton's background?'

Chambers sounded a little angry when he replied.

'All right, Centre, as they say these days – sock 'em to me. The full facts about Joe Acton.'

Centre felt that he was getting into a situation that was difficult, but one which he couldn't avoid now.

'Acton has served a prison sentence. Not only was he found guilty of almost every fraud in the book against his employers, but he also floated a company which he used to milk his creditors. You may or may not know this – but you can't ignore it. I must advise you that if you allow Acton to get involved in your business dealings you will be unwise, and you will be asking for trouble. His status and credit in the locality will be low and he has a bad name. If you wish to make a success of the Sandhill venture–'

'Aw, don't sound so bloody pompous, Centre. It doesn't become you. Look, I know all about Joe Acton. I know that he was a bloody fool some years back. All right, so he fiddled his books. He's also wiped the slate clean, you know that? He's done his time. So why get the knife in again? All I'm concerned about is that I need Joe Acton, and he's fixed me up good. I want him in my company, because he knows his way around. He's already smoothed my path in this business in more ways than one; and it was he who got Karel Martin to promise financial backing for the development – and Martin doesn't throw his money away these days. So don't try to tell me that I've picked a loser.'

'Chambers, I–'

'And while I'm on my high horse, Centre, just one more thing. I like you, old son, I like you and I think that you're a damn smart lawyer. But get a little smarter. I gather that some character has been sniffing around; now it could be that he's your dog, and it could be that he isn't. But if he does belong to you, call him off, or he'll end up on the pavement. I'm saying no more than that: call him off before there's trouble. We could have a beautiful working relationship, Centre – it would be a shame for you to spoil it.'

He rang off before Centre could reply.

Centre stared at the telephone in his hand. He felt vaguely foolish, for he had been caught out in a sense, in that Paul Iles's enquiries must have become obtrusive. He replaced the telephone.

Chambers … and Acton. He stared, unseeingly, at his desk. Don Chambers, out at the Eltham site, had said that Harry Kirk had deserved to die. Acton had been prosecuted by Harry Kirk and would have had little cause to love him.

Now Harry Kirk, the man who had opposed the Sandhill Development, was dead and Don Chambers and Acton were going into business together.

It was time to check with Paul Iles.

Iles stretched his legs and lay back in the easy chair, closing his eyes and sighing. He placed the heel of one foot on the toe of the other and wiggled his shoe.

'You know,' he said, 'it would be a symbolic gesture if I were now to remove my shoes and ease my aching feet, but I value your business too much to run the risk of offending you.'

Centre smiled and fished out a bottle of whisky from the cupboard in the kitchen and walked back to the sitting-room. Iles's eyes lit up as Centre said,

'You won't say no.'

'I won't indeed. A cosy pad, and a glass of the juice is just what I need. I'm glad in a way that you couldn't reach me this afternoon, so we had to make it your flat for a meeting.'

'You were out on the job?'

'I was indeed. And while I'm reviving, you can take a look at the results of my ... ah ... researches. They're there, in the two envelopes that I've placed on your settee.'

'It would seem,' Centre said, walking across to the settee, 'that Chambers at least became aware of your researches.'

'Now is that so?' Iles's battered face was creased with a frown. 'You've now offended my professional pride. Chambers... I've not really got close to him yet. There must be some contact, then, between–'

He paused, ruminating, and scratching his broken nose.

'I'll have to have a little think about that.'

Centre sipped at the whisky he had poured for himself, then set it down to open the first of the two envelopes that Iles had deposited on the settee. It contained a single sheet of paper; it was photocopied material, from some kind of report.

He read it slowly, and with a certain surprise.

'The plaintiff was thirty-eight years of age and a right-handed manual worker. He suffered multiple injuries to the whole of his right arm in an accident while at work. His right elbow, wrist, thumb and fingers are all permanently impaired in function. His right elbow movement is limited to from 130 degrees to 65 degrees, his right forearm has only about 20 degrees of possible supination and no pronation, the right thumb and finger functions are also seriously impaired and he retains only about 20 degrees of the power of his right arm.'

Centre looked up in puzzlement at Iles, but the enquiry agent was devoting the whole of his attention to his drink. Centre returned to the photocopy.

'He has a scar on top of his shoulder, his

right humerus exhibits lateral bowing, movements of the right elbow are grossly restricted, and there is a definite risk that he will later develop osteoarthritis in the right elbow. He is permanently unfit to return to the work he was doing at the time of the accident.'

Centre looked up again to see Iles regarding him thoughtfully, his boxer's head sunk between his broad shoulders.

'What's this all about?' queried Centre.

Iles permitted himself a small smile of satisfaction.

'I'm all for the dramatic effect. That report is the medical evidence which was given in respect of one William John Lawson, of whose existence I was unaware until a certain ...ah ... contact mentioned him to me. Lawson was a dryerman, working in the paper department, when he caught his hand between the two rollers in the machine. The whole of his arm was drawn in and he suffered the injuries you've just read about.'

'So?'

'So the case was settled out of court. £2000 damages, or compensation, or whatever you want to call it.'

'I'm still waiting for the punchline.'

'I admire your patience, but I won't be rushed. Fact is, Lawson took the cash, settled out of court, then ran through the money in just under six months. Wine, women – your

201

Puritan outlook will be satisfied to learn that he is unmarried – and song. He then decided that he hadn't been paid enough so he came running back, complaining to his employer, noising it around that he had been swindled. His employer was a hard man; threatened him with a suit for slander and pointed out, somewhat forcefully, that the matter had already been settled. As it had.'

Centre waited. Iles settled back in his chair with a satisfied grunt.

'His employer,' he added, 'was Harry Kirk.'

'I see,' Centre said softly.

'Not all.' Iles replaced his glass on the small table in front of him and linked his hands comfortably behind his head. 'William John Lawson is also a witness for the prosecution in the case against Stephen Kirk.'

The room was silent. Centre stared at the paper in his hand.

'Interesting,' he murmured.

'I thought you'd find it so. As far as I can make out, Lawson will be testifying as to Stephen Kirk's whereabouts on the night that Harry Kirk died. It is an interesting coincidence, isn't it, that–'

'–that a witness for the prosecution should be a man who had a grudge against Harry Kirk.'

'There's another envelope,' said Iles with some satisfaction.

Centre opened the second envelope. It contained a photograph, six inches by eight, glossy, photoflash, taken in a bar. It featured a man standing with his arm around a blonde, frank-eyed woman. Both seemed to be enjoying the sensation of nearness; both showed open pleasure. The man was tall, well set, greying, with a charming smile and warm drunken eyes. Centre stared at the man ... there was something familiar about him, and yet he could swear that he had never seen him before. He switched his attention to the woman. Her face, her eyes, he recognized them.

'Mrs Lorey,' he said after a moment. 'The wife of Alderman Lorey.'

He remembered the way her glance had flicked around the room, restlessly, at the Law Society dinner.

'I take it,' Centre said when Iles made no attempt to explain, 'that this photograph has some significance.'

'It does. It was taken about eighteen months ago, when the two parties in the photograph were seeing rather a lot of each other, in the literal, it would seem, as well as the metaphorical sense.'

'So?'

Iles was not to be hurried.

'When this photograph was taken there was a dance at Coram Hall. You might know it, it's just out on the–'

'I know it.'

'Yes. Well, this photograph was taken in the bar. It could not have been too long before there occurred what might be described as a scuffle in the garden. It was a warm evening, you know, and there was a full moon, and the Alderman, that respected pillar of our society, walked in the garden and came across his wife, Sandra, and the gentleman you see in the picture. There was a ... er ... discussion, you might say, of a somewhat violent nature. I'm not sure even that blows were not struck.'

'How did you–'

'The photograph is one taken by a newspaper photographer, but it was never printed.'

'Hushed up?'

'Suppressed.'

Centre stared again at the photograph.

'I'll take your punchline from you.'

'I was sure you'd guessed.'

'The man in the dinner-jacket is Harry Kirk.'

It accounted for his half recognition of the photograph – Centre seemed to remember Janet once telling him that Harry and John Kirk had looked alike.

He placed the photograph on the settee and reached for his drink.

'What conclusion do I draw from all this?'

Iles shrugged and smiled.

'That's up to you, Mr Centre. All I'm doing is a little bit of sniffing around. You ask me to get some background on Harry Kirk. That's what I've been after. I can tell you that he wasn't popular. I can tell you that a number of local people didn't like him because he was a foreigner who came in and made good, who pushed himself in local society, who tried to out-English the English, and who threw his money around too flamboyantly. I can tell you that he kicked his son out of his firm, that he prosecuted a man called Acton, and that he made an enemy of an unforgiving character called Lawson. I can tell you that of recent years at least he gave his wife a rough time, and that he played around, most notably with one Sandra Lorey, of fame. But as to what you make of it all, well, your guess, as they say, is as good as mine.'

'I'd like to hear your guess.'

Iles shook his head.

'Too early. There's more stuff I need to get, yet. But I will say this: Lawson hated Harry's guts, and was warned off the estate at Kirkley at least once. And Lorey – well, no one is over fond of being cuckolded. Particularly, publicly.'

Centre stared at his drink. He wondered about Harry Kirk. The man was dead, but his character was now being revealed. The man who had fled from Germany and married Magda; who had become a successful businessman against all the odds, who had forced his way into Linchester society, who had grown rich discarded his son, taken a mistress, prosecuted the accountant who had stolen from him and who had doubtless made many dislike if not hate him, was now having his life shredded, picked over. He had died in a fire and his life was now under the microscope. What else would there be to discover about the man called Harry Kirk?

'Don Chambers,' he said thoughtfully, finishing his whisky. 'Did you find anything on him?'

Iles grimaced.

'Yes, and no. A suspicion … and since he seems to have taken the trouble to speak to you about my investigating him, perhaps my suspicions are justified. I don't know.'

'What have you got so far?'

'Well, he's been not only a big business-man, but a successful one. He started life as a builder on the east coast, and did a nice little line in flats. In the sixties he latched on to the property boom and made himself a moderate pile, and moved out into the development field. Burned his fingers, just once, over a development around Grimsby way, and after that came south. His problem of recent years would seem to have been capital. He's got the ideas, and the flair, but he doesn't impress bankers.'

He paused while Centre refilled his whisky glass, and sighed in content.

'Great... Now then, Chambers ... well, he certainly got some backing for his Sandhill Down project, when he first mooted the idea, but the backers fled after eighteen months passed and no progress was made. The scheme was stymied by the planning committee.'

'But it's been passed now, and he's got backing.'

'That's the point.'

'I don't see it.'

'The scheme went through the planning committee like a dose of salts – *after Harry Kirk died.*'

'You're trying to say–'

'Ah, ah!' Iles wave an admonitory finger. 'Don't put words in my mouth. I'm saying that Harry Kirk was chairman of the planning committee and vociferously and influentially against the Sandhill Down development; I'm saying that as soon as Harry Kirk died the scheme went through. *Alacriter.*'

He grinned.

'Didn't know I was a classical scholar, did you? I tell you Tacitus once spouted out of my ears–'

'So you think there might be–'

Iles shook his head.

'Again, I refuse to think until I've got more

facts. You are rushing me, Mr Centre – you're bitten by the sleuthing bug. You'll start running a temperature soon. Now I'm still looking into the whole deal. I've got a minion ploughing through the council minutes and the reports of the planning committee meetings for the last three years – ever since the Sandhill Down thing came up. They might give us something.'

Centre grunted moodily.

'There's something that they won't tell you. They won't mention that Chambers will be setting up a company to run the scheme, and that Joseph Acton will be one of the directors.'

He had the satisfaction of seeing Iles sit up in surprise, his eyes wide in his battered face.

'You say so! Acton! What the hell is Chambers playing at? He knows all about Acton... Mmm, this bears looking into further.'

He was lost in thought for a while, sipping his whisky and hardly aware that he was doing so. Centre was getting to know Iles well enough to realize that this attitude at least was uncharacteristic: Iles believed in treating good whisky with respect.

'Chambers...' murmured Iles, 'and Acton... Interesting. Have you noticed, Centre, that with all these people there's a sort of focal point around which they revolve? Harry Kirk.'

'It hadn't escaped my attention,' Centre replied.

And yet was it relevant? He was discussing with Paul Iles a number of people who had in some way been involved with Harry Kirk, and most of whom would seem to have had little love for the man. But was this relevant to the defence of a young man charged with murder? Should not David Centre be looking for some way to prove that Stephen could not have committed the act, rather than looking for others who might have been motivated towards murdering Harry Kirk?

He slumped down on the settee.

'Well,' he said, 'we'll know more when we hear the case for the prosecution.'

'Maybe,' replied Iles. 'Who are you briefing?'

'A junior called Corey.'

'I hear he's a good man. When is the preliminary hearing?'

'Day after tomorrow.'

Iles shook his head.

'Time is short – though a committal won't be the end of the world.'

'That's not the way I like to look at it.'

'You may have to.'

There was a flatness about the statement that caused Centre to glance quickly in Iles's direction. The rugged face was expressionless and Iles was staring into his depleted glass silently. There was something important about that silence, something telling, and Centre suddenly realized that Iles, the showman, hadn't finished his act yet. He still had something else to tell David Centre.

'You think,' Centre prompted, 'that we're going to have a tough job in court.'

Iles finished his whisky.

'Damned tough. He still hasn't helped you, Stephen Kirk? Not told you yet where he was the night his parents died?'

'No. He's told me all about the row he had with his father seven years ago, but he still says nothing about the night they died. Do you know where he was?'

'Me? No, wouldn't I have told you if I knew where he was? But the prosecution say they know.'

He stood up and pushed his hands into his pockets. He stared down at Centre.

'The prosecution,' he remarked with precision, 'will produce evidence that would seem to link Stephen Kirk directly with the fire at Kirkley Hall. They will produce witnesses, I gather, to show that he was in Linchester that night. They will try to prove that he actually went to Kirkley Hall that night. Yet he still hasn't given you his side of the story.'

'*You* give it to me.'

'I can't. I don't know it. But next time you see him ... tomorrow?'

'Yes.'

'Next time you see him, Mr Centre—'

It was what Iles had been building up to for the last few minutes, but when it came it fell strangely flat to Centre's ears.

'—ask him to comb his hair.'

3

Centre glared angrily at Stephen Kirk, and the young man wore a worried frown as he returned the glance. He seemed strangely defenceless, but he had been wasting Centre's time and making things more difficult for himself and Centre was not disposed to waste any more time. He reached out a hand to push back the lock of hair that fell over Kirk's forehead, but Stephen drew his head back as though stung.

'What's the matter?' he cried.

'I want to see it,' Centre said.

'Want to see what?' queried Janet, with surprise in her voice as she moved towards them as though to prevent open conflict.

'I want to see the scar!'

Stephen's eyes were round with disbelief. When he spoke his voice was a hoarse, emotional whisper.

'You … you know about it. Who told you?'

'What the hell difference does it make who told me? The fact is that *you* should have

211

told me yourself, long before now! Don't you realize that this isn't a game, that you're facing a charge of murder? Don't you realize that you must tell me everything, whether you think it's relevant or not? Now for God's sake, let me see that scar!'

Reluctantly, a white-faced Stephen Kirk allowed Centre's fingers to lift the lock of hair and explore the scalp. Centre was aware that one of the reasons why Stephen had said nothing about this previously could have been embarrassment – he would not want Janet, among others, to know that he wore a hairpiece – but Centre couldn't worry about things like that. He had a problem.

The reason for the hairpiece lay beneath his fingers at the front of Stephen's head. Centre touched it gently: a scar, long and white, puckered and unpleasant. Around it the hair had refused to grow and Stephen had found it necessary to resort to an artificial lock to cover the unsightly bald mark.

Calmly, Centre sat down.

'Tell me about it.'

Stephen hesitated, and glanced towards Janet, but she was not looking at him. His attention drifted towards the window and the sky and for a moment Centre thought that he was going to lose his concentration again, as he had done on the other, previous occasions, at the trial, and in the bar of the

Callender Hotel.

'Go on,' said Centre harshly, and Stephen looked back to him. When he spoke, his voice held an edge of strain.

'I worked in London for about five years – as an accountant. I had a flat up in Hampstead and had to travel in, but it wasn't until about two years ago that I bought a motorcycle, as transport to work. I hadn't had it all that long when–'

He swallowed hard.

'I was late getting home from work that night. It was January and there was black ice on the road. I was driving home when this car came around the corner, almost three feet over the white line. He pulled back as soon as he saw me, and I suppose there was never any real danger of his hitting me, but instinctively I touched my brakes – you know how one does. It was a mistake: I skidded, the bike hit the kerb, careered into a lamp-post and I went head forward straight into the wall.'

His eyes were vacant suddenly.

'I wasn't wearing a crash helmet. So I was lucky to get out of it alive.'

Janet was silent, her head lowered, taking notes as Centre had asked. He wouldn't need the notes but he wanted her occupied.

'I spent about two months in hospital,' continued Stephen, 'but it was a good five months before I could get back to work. In the meanwhile, a firm had come to me and offered to negotiate with the insurance company for the other driver: I accepted, the case never went to court, but they settled on a payment of £750. They said, after all, I was also to blame. I don't know. Anyway ... at first my head was covered with a sort of skull cap, but when the wound from the operation healed I bought a hairpiece. No one notices, usually. But you noticed...'

'No. I was told, by an enquiry agent, about the operation. He'd checked with your employers and with the hospital, and got the tale from them. He told me you didn't stay long with your employers afterwards ... and that you'd not been employed for about eight months before your parents died.'

Stephen grimaced.

'The doctors – they warned me that I would not be able to take work involving any mental strain. They told me I'd have to take it easy. They were right. I found that there were occasions when I just drifted off – almost like going to sleep. I had tablets – these here, which helped.'

Centre glanced at Janet and she met his glance. They could guess now why Stephen had left them at the Callender Hotel. He had had an attack. And the other occasion in the courtroom ... and indeed it accounted for the feeling that they had both had about Stephen, that there were times when he seemed only to be half listening, when he had seemed unconcerned about matters of some importance.

'The attacks,' said Centre slowly, 'are they regular?'

'No.'

'Do they come – would I be right in suggesting that they are more likely to occur when you are upset, worried about something? Such as the Karnowski suit, for instance?'

'It would seem so.'

Centre contemplated his client. Then, with a swift involuntary look in Janet's direction, he asked,

'What had upset you then, just before your parents died in that fire? Was it just the fact of returning to Linchester?'

Stephen's eyes flickered towards Centre and he opened his mouth to protest; for a second Centre thought that Stephen was going to issue his previous denial. Instead, he paused, then shrugged and capitulated. He had decided to give up the struggle.

'No. I'd better tell you what happened. At least, all that I can remember. I ... I lied to you earlier. I did come back to Linchester, I came back on the day my parents died.'

Centre made no movement and did not look in Janet's direction though he was conscious of her eyes on him. He wanted no cheap victories at her expense.

'What made you come back?'

'I … I received a letter from my father.'

'*Harry Kirk wrote to you?*'

Stephen nodded abstractedly.

'He wrote that he wanted to see me. It simply said that he wanted me to come out to Kirkley. No reason given. Just to call to see him.'

'Where is the letter now?'

'I don't know. I've looked for it… I intended burning it, I don't know. But I can't find it, I've no idea what happened to it.'

Centre pondered for a moment, his eyes on Stephen. He gained the impression that this time at least the young man was telling the truth.

'All right,' he said. 'You received the letter from your father. What then?'

'I didn't know what to do. I hadn't heard a word from any of them – from him or my mother or any of them for seven years. I don't even know how he could have found my address–'

'These things are not so difficult,' Centre said. Moreover, he thought, the hospital would probably have got in touch with Harry Kirk when Stephen was involved in the accident. But the man had done nothing. Centre wondered whether he could have told Magda about her son's injuries. He guessed not – Magda would surely have got in touch with Stephen had that been the case. Centre's lip curled; Harry Kirk had been a hard man, keeping the knowledge of his own son's serious accident from his wife. But why then had he written?

'Anyway, I came down to Linchester that very day.'

'The fifteenth of June?'

'That's right. I was in a bit of a state. In a way I didn't want to see him, but I had to come. I was scared, and worried in case he was going to have another go at me. And after seven years it was a bit unnerving, getting that letter. But I had to come...'

Nervously he brushed the lock of hair back from his forehead.

'And there was the thought of Mother ... how she'd be upset... Anyway, I booked into a hotel in Linchester – under an assumed name, Cornish, don't ask me why, it just seemed right at the time. I didn't want anyone to know I was in town, you know? It ... it just seemed important. Maybe I felt that if I changed my mind I could then turn tail and run back to London and none would be the wiser.'

'All right. You booked into the hotel–'

'And I stayed there in my room until teatime.'

'Then?'

Stephen spread his hands.

'I felt hungry. About six, I left the hotel and went for a meal. It must have been about seven-thirty when I finished the meal and the evening stretched ahead of me–'

'Now wait a minute. What had your father's note said – about seeing him, I mean?'

Stephen grunted.

'Oh, he was as meticulous as ever. He wanted me to call at 11 a.m.'

'On the fifteenth?'

'No. Next day.'

'I see. Well, after your meal that evening, what did you do?'

'I just wandered around for a bit. Had a drink, a few drinks in fact. Then went back to the hotel.'

'Is that all?'

'I think so.'

'What the hell do you mean, you *think* so! I want to know, Stephen, with precision, what you did that evening.'

Stephen was struggling.

'I'm not sure that I can remember–'

'The hell with that! We've been through this game before. Look, I can't take any more of this, Stephen – either you play it straight with me or else you can find some other damned lawyer to handle your case. If I don't get the truth from you how the hell am I supposed to defend you? I want the truth, Stephen, the *truth*.'

This time, Janet was making no protest. There was desperation in Stephen Kirk's eyes.

'All right, all right. I'll tell you. I'll cut my throat in the process, but I'll tell you, and to hell with it. To hell with it all! I went for a drink about seven-thirty or eight, and I drank steadily and pretty solidly. I was in bad shape, I've no doubt, when I left that bar. The next thing I did was to go down to the bus station.'

'You went to Kirkley Hall.'

'Yes. Don't ask me why. I was half cut – maybe that was why. Perhaps there were other reasons – I was upset, scared, I wanted to see the place again, maybe I thought that if I looked in through the windows I'd see Mother, or see him, and perhaps decide to call it a day, take the next train back. I don't know. All I do know is that I was drawn there that night and I went there.'

'What happened then?'

Stephen hesitated, eyeing Centre uncertainly.

'I've held back a good deal from you, Mr Centre, and I'm sorry. I should have told you all this before, but I was scared. It puts me in a bad light. So I told you I couldn't remember. It was a feeble attempt to … well, to put off the evil hour, I suppose. That's all.'

'Well, tell me it all now.'

'I can't.'

Centre began to bridle, then hesitated, watching Stephen carefully.

'Why not? Why can't you tell me what

happened at Kirkley Hall?'

'Because I can't remember.'

The room was silent as Centre and Janet stared at Stephen Kirk. He could not meet their eyes, he stared at his hands, and yet David Centre felt that this time the man was telling the truth. He had no further reason to prevaricate.

'All right, Stephen, just tell me what you *can* remember that evening.'

'You believe me,' muttered Stephen in some surprise.

'Just tell me what you can remember,' repeated Centre.

It was curious; a gleam of hope had appeared in Stephen's face. It was as though he felt that if he could convince Centre he could convince others too, and his cause was not completely lost.

'Well, I remember getting pretty tight–'

And that, thought Centre, with his mental condition anyway, wouldn't help very much.

'–and then getting the bus out to Linchester. I remember walking up the drive, and walking around the house. There were lights on upstairs, I remember that. After that, there are hazy recollections only. I know I must have fallen at some point because my hip was grazed, and there was a bruise on my face, but where, and against what I have no idea.'

'There's nothing else that you can remember?'

Stephen seemed distressed.

'I can remember getting a lift back to Linchester. I flagged a car down in the road – it was a commercial traveller who gave me a lift. He dropped me near the hotel.'

'But what about the interim period – between the time you arrived at Kirkley Hall and the time you obtained the lift?'

Stephen shook his head.

'I remember the drive, and the door...'

'Nothing else? Was there nothing else?' Centre asked persistently.

In the car, on the way back to the office, Janet looked at Centre as though trying to read his thoughts. Finally, she asked him outright.

'What do you think of Stephen's chances?'

'I just can't say, Janet. It's one hell of a situation that he finds himself in.'

'But if he can't remember what happened – I mean, can they just go ahead?'

Centre frowned, and shook his head.

'The prosecution will have witnesses, no doubt, as to Stephen's presence in Linchester, and maybe at Kirkley Hall too. The fact that he's unable to give us a coherent account of what happened when he was there will make little difference.'

Janet disagreed vehemently.

'If he can't say what happened, because of this trouble he gets with his head, induced by his wound, how can he be expected to defend himself properly? Surely, if he can't say what happened that makes a difference? I mean he might well have the perfect answer to the charges, if only he wasn't afflicted with this dreadful–'

'You're convinced he didn't kill them?'

'Of course. Aren't you?'

'He had the motive – no job, the realization that he would inherit the family fortune, and the opportunity – he admits to having gone there that night. Moreover, his state of mind could hardly be described as *balanced* and it would seem that he was more than a little drunk.'

'I'm sure that all this is what the prosecution will say, but you don't believe it any more than I do.'

'I just don't know, Janet. He was ill, upset, and he was out there... I just don't know what to believe.'

Janet was silent for a little while and there was only the muted roar of the engine of the Aston Martin and the whistle of the wind to disturb their private thoughts. Finally, she asked,

'If he truly can't remember would you not be able to argue that he *could* have a complete defence but is unable to bring it because of his memory? Would you not be able to stop proceedings on that basis?'

Centre shook his head.

'It's been tried before.'

'What happened?'

'The Podola Case. The man claimed that he suffered from hysterical amnesia and it went to the Court of Appeal on that issue: could hysterical amnesia prevent him from lodging a plea and therefore render him not liable to prosecution. The court held that a man is fit to plead where hysterical amnesia prevents him from remembering events during the period material to the question whether he committed the crime with which he is charged. Provided, that is, that his mind is otherwise completely normal.'

'Stephen's mind is not normal!'

'Isn't it? It's a moot point, and expert witnesses would be needed to support that contention. He suffers from a form of amnesia but is that enough to suggest that he is abnormal? It won't wash, Janet, but in any case I'm hoping it won't get to that stage. It all depends upon the strength of the case that the prosecution will present tomorrow, in court.'

He fixed his eyes on the curving road ahead and Janet kept any further thoughts to herself. His mind, however, was in a turmoil. The fact was he was no longer sure whether Stephen was innocent or guilty – but had he ever been sure? Hadn't he doubted Stephen almost from the beginning, for his lies, his prevarication, and his deceit? It was true that Stephen had had understandable reasons, according to his own lights, for his actions since his arrest, but that did not materially change the position. The case against Stephen Kirk would unfold tomorrow, but Centre feared the outcome.

He feared it because when he had pressed Stephen this afternoon, pressed him to try to remember what happened between the times of his arrival at Kirkley Hall and his return lift to Linchester, Stephen had stammered, and gone white and finally made a statement that put the issues right out into the open.

'All I can remember,' he had blurted out, 'was the haziness inside my own head, and the lights upstairs ... and then the smoke...'

He had put his head in his hands.

'And then the screaming,' he had whispered.

He had looked up to Centre, with a haggard face.

'The screaming ... that was my mother.'

CHAPTER V

'Hell, hell, hell!'

Blake looked suitably downcast.

'I'm sorry, Mr Centre.'

'Don't be silly, Charles, it's not your fault. But what a time!'

Centre marched angrily through Janet's room and across to his own. He met Janet coming out with a pile of letters that had just arrived that morning. She raised her eyebrows.

'You look black as thunder,' she exclaimed.

Centre wore.

'That blasted man Corey – his clerk has just telephoned to say that he won't be able to appear before the magistrates today. Corey is otherwise engaged!'

'Otherwise engaged? Can he do that? Just cry off at the last moment, I mean?'

'There is nothing to stop him. It would seem that a clash has arisen: he is called to Winchester Assizes earlier than he had anticipated so he has gone – and will be involved there for the rest of the week.'

'But Charles was assured by his clerk at least ten days ago that–'

'Makes no difference, Janet. Corey can do

it, even if the Bar Council frown upon it. I wouldn't be surprised if he even asks for his fee as well.'

'The nerve!' gasped Janet.

'The system,' disagreed Centre.

He walked across the room and dropped into his chair, disconsolately. Blake followed him into the room.

'Corey's clerk offers us Mr Baker, but he's the only one.'

'Baker?'

'Recently completed his pupillage, I understand.'

Centre shook his head positively.

'No, I think we'd better scrub around that. Corey knows the brief. The only thing we can do now is hear out the prosecution case: I'll have a crack at the prosecution witnesses myself and reserve our defence if Stephen Kirk gets committed for trial at the next Assizes. I hope it won't go that far. Anyway, if it does we'll brief Corey then – he's the ablest we'll get for the fee.'

Janet was still standing in the doorway; anger at Corey's defection still flared in her eyes. She was taking the matter as a personal affront. Centre smiled at her.

'Don't worry, Janet, we'll muddle through. You go on back to work; I'd be grateful if you'd keep an eye on things here this afternoon, for I'll want Charles in court with me. Nothing else on your plate, Charles?'

'Just a few of the Eltham conveyances, Mr Centre, but they can be completed later in the week.'

Centre nodded in satisfaction.

'Good. Then we'll get around to the magistrates' court straight after lunch today – just as well that they're starting a bit later than usual. At least it gives us a few hours to get things straight.'

He spent the rest of the morning looking again through the brief that he had prepared for Corey and checking up on a few cases – though he doubted whether he'd need to use them. The brief was pretty thin, in any case. The operation would have to be very much a defensive one – all he could hope to do was to dig a few holes in the prosecution case. There was one exception: Lawson. The man would have to be attacked, there was no doubt about that. The plan of attack would have to wait until he had delivered his evidence, of course.

Centre took no lunch. Janet slipped out for a sandwich herself and returned with a few ham rolls which he munched with the cup of coffee that she prepared for him. At one-thirty Charles Blake knocked at the door to see if he was ready.

He was.

They walked across the town centre and through the square to the magistrates' court. There was a small knot of people outside and

Centre was surprised since he had expected more, but then he realized that most people had already gone inside into the public seats. The case was inevitably going to be something of a *cause célèbre;* Harry Kirk had been well known and it wasn't often that a Linchester resident was murdered.

The junior engaged for the prosecution was already there. His name was Stanley. He was a short, angular man with high cheekbones and deep-set eyes. His face was pale, his mouth lined; he had made a reputation as a quick-witted advocate and one who took advantage of every opening offered. He had started late at the Bar, later in life than was customary, at least, but it was said that he might well take silk within the next few years, if only to achieve a less hectic life. Centre was not surprised; the man looked ill – probably worn out by the pressure of a successful career as a junior. Fees might be high, but the good men worked for them, there was no doubt about that.

Stephen also looked ill. His face twitched and the tell-tale vacant look drifted into his eyes twice as Centre spoke with him, trying to calm him as much as possible. Centre had little success in his efforts and this worried him; it was true that Stephen would not be giving evidence this time but if the case went to the Assizes and Stephen was called there, the impression he would give would be far from favourable.

Charles Miles, JP, was Chairman of the Bench. He was flanked by Edwards, a brewery manager who had been active in the Youth Service and who retained a sort of bouncy enthusiasm on the Bench, and Acland, a retired headmaster who had worked at the local direct grant school and had been prominent in local politics as an Independent of Conservative leanings. He was reputed to have an acid tongue, thought it was unlikely it would find expression on this occasion since preliminary investigations tended to have an inhibiting effect upon the garrulity of magistrates.

Stephen sat very still while the opening speech for the prosecution was made. Centre listened hard; the speech was a workmanlike one, lacking histrionics and the more effective for all that. It would impress Miles and his fellow justice – they wouldn't want 'lawyers' nonsense'.

Stanley stated that the prosecution would prove that Stephen Kirk was present at Kirkley Hall on June fifteenth, that he had fired the house and was thus responsible for the deaths of his parents, and that his prime motivations were revenge and gain: revenge upon his father for his dismissal, and sparked now by his own reduced circumstances, and gain in the sense that he hoped to profit from the death of his parents by inheriting the estate.

Centre was aware of the tremor that ran through Stephen Kirk; it distracted him from the ephemeral thought that had suddenly touched his mind. It was gone now – and the first witness was being called.

Her name was Mrs Henson.

David Centre turned to his client and Stephen whispered, 'It's the woman who keeps the hotel – where I stayed, you know.'

Centre nodded grimly. It was a bad start in the sense that it showed that the prosecution had done its homework. Stanley was moving forward in a curious mincing gait to question the witness. Centre stared at her dispassionately: there would be very little that he could do about this short, dumpy, red-haired and probably patently honest woman.

'You are Mrs Gladys Henson and you keep the hotel known as the Fortune Hotel in Little Gladstone Street?'

'That's right, sir.'

'Perhaps you would be so kind, Mrs Henson, as to tell the Court what happened on the night of June fifteenth.'

'Yes, sir. Well, I was sitting in the lounge of my private quarters, you know, and I'd just made a cupper. There was this programme on the telly about birth control and with me being a Catholic and all that, well, I didn't really think I ought to be watching it, because the Father–'

230

'Yes, yes, Mrs Henson, but perhaps–?'

'Oh yes, sir. Of course. I walked through the hotel lounge to see if there was anything I could help out with in the reception or the dining-room but of course it was all quiet and then–'

'One moment, Mrs Henson – might I ask why you are so certain that these were your movements on the night in question?'

'The date, you mean? How did I know this what I'm about to say happened on June the fifteenth? Well, you see, I was feeling a bit down because it was the anniversary of the date that our Joan ran away from home and I haven't seen her since, you know. What with that and–'

'Thank you, Mrs Henson. You said that you went out of your own private quarters, and then?'

'Well, I had a chat with Millie who was just putting on her coat because she'd finished the washing up in the bar and was off to catch her bus.'

'Her … ah … transport left at what time?'

'Last bus, it was – half past eleven.'

'Please go on.'

'Well, Millie went off and I looked on the board to see if everyone was in before I locked up. I could see that there was two still out. Now Billy York was one, and he's a commercial gent who's stayed with me often and is always late in from the tiles if you know what I mean, so I'd given him his own key anyway. But the other, this Mr Cornish, it was the first time he'd stayed with me and so I thought I'd better wait up for a while to let him in, and so on. Didn't want to be knocked up once I was in my bed.'

'Did you have to wait long?'

'Till about half past twelve. I heard him coming in and I was just dozing. I heard his steps in the hall.'

'Did you come out to greet him?'

Mrs Henson was very positive with her hands clasped together across her stomach and a determined, slightly disapproving look in her eye.

'Oh yes. I didn't like the way he was sort of scuffling in the hall. I thought that perhaps he was a bit squiffy.'

'You mean intoxicated?'

'S'right. Squiffy.'

'And was he … ah … intoxicated?'

Centre half rose, regarding the question improper, but sank back as Mrs Henson continued.

'Oh, I couldn't say that, sir. How do I know? Some people, you can't tell, you can't, can you? But this Mr Cornish, he was more tired than tight, if you ask me. He was leaning against the wall. He was sort of gasping for breath and I said something to him, asking if he was all right but he sort of looked right through me and then mumbled something and pushed past me. Pushed me aside in fact and went on up to his room. I was a bit upset really, the way he behaved.'

'Was there anything about his appearance that attracted your attention?'

She nodded emphatically.

'The sleeve of his jacket was torn and he had a mark, like a smear of blood, on his face.' She paused. 'There was a funny smell, too.'

'What did it remind you of?'

'Woodsmoke.'

'Tell me, Mrs Henson,' said Stanley smoothly, a little smile flickering across his lips. 'This Mr Cornish – would you recognize him again?'

'Oh yes, indeed, sir. That's him – over there!'

She pointed a stubby finger straight at Stephen Kirk.

Stanley waved a deprecating hand and sat down. Charles Miles humphed and Acland coughed. Centre proceeded to cross-examination. It was hopeless. There was nothing in her account that he could shake since it was all largely factual and she possessed the indignation of a person who is telling the truth. After a desultory attempt to discredit her memory he attempted to attack her suggestion that she would be able to detect the smell of smoke on his clothing but she insisted upon the sensitivity of her sense of smell and refused to budge. As he sat down, Centre wondered whether there had been any point in cross-examination anyway since Stephen would have to admit to his presence there at the hotel – though he hadn't mentioned his encounter with Mrs Henson. Still, there were many things that Stephen seemed not to have mentioned.

The next witness called was a man called Crossley. He was a commercial traveller; it transpired that he was the man who had given Stephen a lift from Kirkley Hall.

'Why do you say,' asked Centre in cross-examination, 'that you gave him a lift from Kirkley Hall? Did you pick him up outside the house?'

'No, but–'

'Or in the drive, or at the end of the drive?'

'No, sir, I–'

'Or was it some distance down the road?'

'Well, it was about a half mile, actually, sir, from the end of the drive. In the Linchester direction.'

'So you couldn't *say*, in fact, that he had been at Kirkley Hall?'

'Well, no, I couldn't, but it seems reasonable to suppose–'

'Supposition, Mr Crossley, is not evidence!'

But there was little comfort to be gained out of that interchange, for Crossley had also testified to Stephen's wild appearance, and to his incoherence, and to the fact that he had dropped him near the Fortune Hotel at about twelve-twenty on June fifteenth. And in any case, the question of Stephen's presence at Kirkley Hall was introduced into evidence by the next witness.

'Your name,' said Stanley in his precise tones, 'is William John Lawson, of Church Cottages, Linchester?'

The man facing Stanley nodded. He was short, with greying hair that was worn long at the nape of his neck and his sideburns reached down to his jawline. He wore a dark suit that was of an expensive cut but somewhat the worse for wear. His shirt was white, a little grubby, and the collar was frayed and had been inexpertly trimmed of its cotton ends by a clumsily wielded pair of scissors. His eyes were quick and sharp, his mouth tight. His right arm he kept huddled close to his side.

Stanley led him through his evidence.

'Would you please tell the court of the observations you made on the night of June fifteenth, Mr Lawson.'

Lawson flickered a tongue across dry lips.

'I had been down to the Green Man at Sandhill, with some of the lads. We had a few pints. After stop tap I decided that I'd walk to the bus stop on the 35 route because the last 52 to Linchester had gone.'

'This particular stop,' interrupted Stanley,

'the 35 route stop – where is it, precisely? Did it mean that you were walking away from Linchester?'

'That's right. It's up beyond the junction, where the Sandhill road joins the road between Linchester and Kirkley Hall.'

Centre stared thoughtfully at Lawson: so the man had been walking towards Kirkley Hall, had he?

'The bus stop is about forty yards from the entrance to Kirkley Hall,' continued Lawson. 'I waited for the bus for a little while and sort of walked up and down, strolling like, and after a while I heard the sounds of someone running down the drive from the Hall. He was out of breath and I could hear him kind of sobbing as he came, gasping for air. I don't know why, exactly, but I sort of drew into the side, under the hedge and a few seconds later this chap – he sort of burst out of the drive and came lurchin' and runnin' past me, headed Linchester way.'

'Did you recognize him?'

'No. Not at the time.'

'Do you see him in court?'

'Oh yus. That's him over there. Stephen Kirk.'

'And what time was it that you saw him?'

'About five to twelve. The last bus came along at twelve. I was the only one on it.'

'Did the vehicle pass Mr Kirk on the road?'

'Not that I saw.'

'Thank you, Mr Lawson. Mr Centre?'

Centre rose slowly to his feet and faced Lawson. The man made no attempt to meet his glance.

'Mr Lawson,' said Centre staring coldly at the witness, 'you didn't recognize Stephen Kirk at the time. When did you recognize him? When the police showed you his photograph?'

'No,' said Lawson, with a twisted smile. 'I recognized him in the road – his face I mean – but I couldn't put a name to him. Then. Later, I remembered.'

'How much later?'

'When I heard about him and the Karnowski case. It rang the bell, you know.'

'That's when you went to the police.'

'Yus.'

'Have you seen Stephen Kirk of recent years?'

'No.'

'Not since he left Linchester?'

'No.'

'But you knew him before he left.'

'That's right.'

'What were you doing at the entrance to Kirkley Hall on the night of the fire, Mr Lawson?'

'I said. Waiting for a bus.'

'No other reason?'

'I'd missed the last 52; I was waiting for

the last 35.'

'Did you like Stephen Kirk ... when you knew him?'

Lawson was unable to meet Centre's glance. He twitched his right arm involuntarily.

'I hardly knew him.'

'But you knew his father.'

'I knew Harry Kirk, yus, a lot of people knew him.'

'What was your relationship with Harry Kirk?'

'Relationship? Well, he employed me at one time, that's all.'

'Were you welcome at his house?'

'Dunno. Can't say I ever went there.'

'Wasn't that where you were on the night of June fifteenth?'

Stanley's chair screeched. Lawson's eyes flickered towards the prosecuting attorney.

'I told you. I was waiting for a bus.'

'I think you were going towards Kirkley Hall. You said that you had never been there?'

Stanley rose lazily.

'Your worship, I fail to see–'

'So do I,' agreed Charles Miles, with a frown.

'There is a purpose in my cross-examination,' Centre said, looking up to Miles. 'I am interested, sir, in Mr Lawson's real reasons for being in the vicinity – it hinges on his connection with the family, and will,

I feel sure, show that little credibility is to be attached to his story.'

Miles shrugged unhappily and Centre turned back to Lawson. The interim period had warned the little man, and his eyes were wary and truculent.

'I repeat the question – would you be welcome at Kirkley Hall?'

'I don't know.'

'Is it not true that you had on at least one occasion been turned away from the Hall, under the threat of a prosecution?'

'You're talking rot.'

'You mean you never went to Kirkley Hall in pursuit of what you regarded as your lawful and just remedy against Harry Kirk? And that you were not on your way there that night? Or perhaps you had already paid a visit there at the time you mention – midnight?'

Stanley's chair was screeching again but Centre was launched.

'You knew Stephen Kirk because you worked with him; you were both employees, though in different departments, of Harry Kirk. You knew the family because you threatened to sue them, but settled out of court. You have reason to dislike the whole family because you thought later that you'd been swindled and you pressed Harry Kirk for more. That was why you went, at least once, to Kirkley Hall and were thrown off the premises. What I want to know is did you continue to press Harry Kirk after that?'

'No.'

'Did you continue to prowl around the Hall? Did you continue to spy out the place in the hope that you could get at Harry Kirk?'

'No!'

'That was why you were there that night, wasn't it? You went to Kirkley Hall to demand more money. You didn't see Stephen Kirk at all, did you?'

'I was in the road, and I saw—'

'Or were you in the drive, or up at the Hall? Or was it just that your hatred for Harry Kirk conjured the vision of Stephen Kirk to your mind?'

There was a sudden silence in the courtroom. Lawson was glaring angrily at Centre, but his lips were clamped shut. He was in complete control, and so was Stanley. Centre suddenly realised that he had done his own, and Stephen's, cause no good by attacking Lawson. Stanley had allowed it to happen, quite deliberately, and now reaped the reward.

'I am amazed, your worship,' he was saying. 'Absolutely amazed at the conduct of the defence. If this is the only method that can be devised to defend the accused one can only draw the obvious conclusions. I would remind your worship that it is the accused who is on trial, not this witness. Moreover, the affidavits placed before the court amply demonstrate that the witness certainly was in the Green Man earlier, and could not have been, as my learned friend suggests, at Kirkley Hall. He would simply not have had the time. However, I assume from my friend's silence that he has concluded his cross-examination. If that is the case, I will proceed to re-examine Mr Lawson.'

Centre opened his mouth, and closed it again. He had made a mess of the situation – there was no point in making it worse. Glumly, and humiliatingly, he listened to Stanley taking Lawson through the main points of his evidence again. Each point would now strike home like a hammer-blow after the wild and inept cross-examination technique in which David Centre had indulged.

He was the more furious with himself for the conviction that it was more than mere coincidence that Lawson had been near Kirkley Hall on that particular night, at that particular time.

The next witness was being called.

She was small, buxom and in her late thirties. A slight buzz in the courtroom told him that she was known to more than a few in the public seats. The reason soon became apparent. It seemed that Pat Mason frequented Linchester bars and was not averse to being bought drinks by strangers.

And one such stranger had been Stephen Kirk.

'Oh yes,' she said sweetly. 'He was in the bar that night, really knocking back the whiskies and I told him he'd end up under the tables or somewhere worse if he didn't lay off. He didn't lay off, and the last I saw of him was he was weaving in the direction of the bus station. Oh yes, he said that he wanted a bus out to Sandhill... Said he wanted to have a showdown with his old man. Yes, that's right, those were the words he used. Make him see sense, he said, have a showdown...'

Stanley's manipulation of the witness was effective. Centre declined to cross-examine with any persistence. He obtained the impression that he would shake the lady only with difficulty, and his experience with Lawson had inhibited him somewhat.

The next witness to be called was Joseph, the butler employed by the Kirks. He gave evidence that he had been in his room when he had heard Mrs Kirk screaming. He had run out into the main wing and seen the upper house in flames. It was Joseph who had telephoned for the fire brigade – they had taken almost fifteen minutes to arrive and Harry and Magda Kirk had been charred beyond recognition.

'What was the point of all that?' asked Stephen in a worried voice. He was obviously much affected by the man's account of the fire.

'It's simply establishing the time of death,' said Centre, unwilling to spell out the whole story for Stephen. But the pieces were fitting into place. The Kirks had died at about 11.50, and it had been established that Stephen Kirk had come to Linchester that morning, had got drunk in a bar in the evening and stated that he wanted to make his father see sense, and had been seen running away from Kirkley Hall at 11.55 to arrive in a dishevelled condition at his hotel at about 12.30 a.m.

The court was rising, and Centre was wondering what the next morning would bring by way of further damaging evidence. One thing was for sure: the cross-examinations would not be handled more ineptly than they had been today.

Stanley must be getting pretty sure of a committal. The circumstantial evidence was building up against Stephen Kirk, effectively and damningly. And the only answer that he had was that he just couldn't remember.

Centre got back to the office just before five. Janet was there, and her brown eyes softened when she saw the expression on his face.

'Could you use a cup of coffee?'

'I could.'

She returned a few minutes later with the

coffee. He was slumped in his chair, head back, eyes closed.

'I made a right mess of it, Janet.'

'I'm sure you did your best,' Janet replied quietly, placing the coffee cup on his desk.

'Wasn't good enough. Things look bad. The prosecution seem to have it closely tied up.'

'How ... how is Stephen?'

Centre wondered about the fractional hesitation, but felt a rush of sympathy for the girl. He had momentarily forgotten the friendship that had sprung up between Janet and Stephen – indeed, for all he knew, they could be lovers. He sat up and sipped his coffee. Stephen would be a lucky man, if that were the case.

If he escaped sentence.

'He's facing up reasonably well. Much will depend upon what happens tomorrow, of course, but I don't think he had any illusions about today. And my handling of it didn't help. He should have got a criminal lawyer, not a country bumpkin.'

'He wanted a sympathetic man,' Janet demurred, 'and he got one.'

He stared at her for a moment – there had been something in her tone... He brushed the thought aside, it was silly.

'By the way,' she continued, 'I'd not told you. Mr Iles telephoned – he wants you to ring him as soon as you come in.'

'Which is now. I'll do it right away. Er ... Charles should be in shortly, Janet – I'm sure he'd appreciate a cup of coffee from your fair hand also.'

'Of course, Mr Centre.'

Centre rang Iles's number. Iles picked up the telephone immediately.

'Ah, Mr Centre – how did things go today?'

Centre told him, succinctly, and without prevarication as to his own part in the proceedings. Iles grunted noncommittally.

'However,' said Centre, 'I gather you wanted me to get in touch?'

'That's right. Things have been moving during the last forty-eight hours – since we last talked. You'll remember, I refused to make any guesses then.'

'You are now?'

'I think so. I'd like you to call around at the bungalow this evening, Mr Centre. I've asked a certain party to visit me there, and I think it would be useful and instructive for you to be there also, in a conveniently hidden position. He'll be coming to the bungalow to explain to me just where he was on the night that Harry Kirk died.'

'From which I gather–'

'From which you gather that I think I know who murdered Harry Kirk.'

It was cold and he was shivering. Or was it merely the fact that the night air touched his skin? Maybe it was the suppressed excitement as he stood just outside the half-open window, in the shadow of the bungalow, with the long grass of the lawn dampening his ankles. The light from the window cut sharply across the lawn to his right, but from where he stood he could see straight into the room, could see the two men standing there near the table, and he could hear every word that they said.

Iles poured out a glass of whisky.

'That is a stiffer drink than I require,' said his visitor.

Iles grinned wolfishly.

'I think you're going to need a stiff drink, Alderman.'

James Lorey took the proffered glass and sipped at it carefully. His heavy features were perfectly composed, his eyes calm as they flickered a glance around the room, weighing up, measuring, reaching decisions. Iles knew that the alderman would be noting that his furniture was inexpensive, that the carpet was cord, not pile, that the pictures were cheap prints, the chair-arms worn, the books paper-backed.

'I'm a busy man,' Lorey said in a soft voice.

'That's one of the reasons why I asked you around to my place.' Iles's battered face was expressionless. 'You see, I've been hearing all about some of the ways in which you've been … er … busying yourself.'

Lorey's calmness would have deceived many.

'I seem to detect some barb there, but I'm not at all clear why the arrow should be pointing in my direction at all. And you say you've been "hearing" – would that be a euphemism for "snooping"?'

'I would prefer simply to state that certain information has come into my hands.'

'Then,' said Lorey pompously, 'you can rest assured that as an alderman of the town council I will do my best to–'

'Oh, you've already done your best, Alderman. And up to now it's been a good best. I'm quite impressed by the way you've managed to manipulate things.'

'I'm not at all sure that we're on the same wavelength, Mr Iles.'

'Oh, we are, you know. After all, you wouldn't have come here if we weren't – my cryptic invitation wouldn't have meant anything to a man who was innocent.'

Lorey set down his glass carefully.

'I think,' he said with precision, 'that from now on we had better start using words with care. Words like "innocent" for instance. Now what precisely are you implying, Iles?'

'Well,' said Iles expansively, 'let's put it this way. I've been asked by a client of mine to look into certain matters – you'll appreciate that I can say no more on ethical grounds. Well, curiously enough, your name cropped up, and seemed to keep cropping up thereafter, more than it should have done. And I was suddenly surprised to find that in a way you've been quite a little businessman – in the land dealing sense.'

He smiled, and waved his whisky glass in an airy gesture of confidence.

'Am I getting through to you, Alderman?'

'Not yet,' Lorey replied, but he had paled.

'Then I'll elaborate further. It just so happened I had occasion to look into the development plan for Sandhill Down. This plan, or scheme if you like, has caused a great deal of trouble locally. The planning committee and the full council have been much concerned over it.'

'So?'

'Well, I looked right back through three years of records and minutes, and it became apparent to me that two factions had developed on the planning committee. In one of those factions, the one standing out in opposition to the development, you were more than vociferous.'

'That's right. I was against the development.'

'Yes. Now the last planning committee

meeting approved the plan, and it has also been approved by the full council. The interesting thing is that you, as the new chairman of the planning committee, were suddenly in favour of the development, both in planning committee and full council.'

'There is nothing curious in that. I changed my mind.'

'And so did a number of other worthy gentlemen, it seems.'

Lorey eyed Iles speculatively for a moment, then shrugged his shoulders.

'I think I'm wasting my time here. I'll take my leave of you, Mr Iles.'

'I think not, Alderman. I haven't given out the whole tale yet.'

'Then do so. I can't hang about here indefinitely.'

Iles grinned, creasing his battered face.

'All right. You fought against that scheme for two years, then suddenly approved it, and a number or your minions followed your lead. Now what happened in the meanwhile, thought I. And then I heard about Crampton House.'

Lorey smiled now, but it was an unpleasant smile which contained no humour.

'I see. So you have discovered that nine months ago I sold Crampton House, which comprises part of the Sandhill Down development area, to a company. I will add that I suppose you have also discovered that at the time of the committee meetings I did not mention this and so acted in contravention of the Local Government Act, 1933, Section 76 – which demands that I declare my interest. All right, so what? If it is taken further and I am fined the £200 I will gladly pay. The point is that this will in no way impugn the decision of committee or council. The decisions stand. Is that all, Mr Iles? Or were you hoping to indulge in some mild blackmail?'

'Oh, not at all, Alderman. You see, you interrupted me. I hadn't finished.'

Iles sighed in his best theatrical manner.

'You see, I know about the £200 fine and all that, but there's more to come, as you well know. You've made, and stand to make, a packet out of all these deals. I mean, the sale of Crampton House was chickenfeed, wasn't it? There's more gold around the corner.'

'I don't know what you mean,' Lorey said thickly.

'Well, we haven't talked about Don Chambers, or Joe Acton or Karel Martin yet, have we?'

Lorey glared, but made no reply.

'You have been a busy little alderman, I know. Full of good works. But you've been lining your own pocket with more industry than you've ever shown in pursuit of the public good. I don't know how long ago it was that you first got tied in with Chambers

– I don't know how long ago, or who it was made the first play. It doesn't matter. I do know that you've been Chambers's man on the council–'

'Don't be absurd.'

Iles regarded the alderman calmly, as he would a recalcitrant child.

'I've *checked*,' he said. 'I can see the picture. Chambers bought you, a long time ago. You and your boys on the committee played it cool, though – you supported the lobby against the development only until the time was ripe, and then to everyone's surprise you moved over, lock and stock. And swung both committee and council in favour of the scheme. And why? Well, I've been digging like the proverbial mole and I come up with interesting facts. My associates in London tell me that Karel Martin – a money-lender of some quality – is backing the Sandhill Down project to the tune of some hundred thousand pounds. I learn that Crampton House was sold to a company floated by a gentleman called Acton. I am told that Acton is going into business with Chambers. Who will be the directors of the development company for the Sandhill Down scheme? Chambers, Acton – and who else, Lorey? You?'

'I don't see–'

'Which brings us back to Karel Martin. He is in the business of lending money – and this is a good scheme. But he must have wanted security for the cash – I understand that bonds were put up as security. Who got the bonds, Lorey? Acton, wasn't it? How will Karel Martin feel when he discovers that those bonds are forged?'

Lorey gasped.

'What are you trying to say–'

'Now, now, don't get hasty. In a rough-house, Alderman, remember I'm as big as and younger than you. Not like Harry Kirk, eh?'

Lorey stood stock still. He bared his teeth.

'What do you mean by that?'

'Oh,' said Iles with an airy wave of his hand, 'you remember the fracas out at Coram Hall, surely. You, and Harry Kirk … and Sandra. You didn't like being openly cuckolded, that was it, wasn't it, Alderman?'

'Iles, I'll break your–'

'Like you did Harry's?'

Lorey took a step towards Iles and then stopped. He stood there solidly, fighting for control of his temper.

'I didn't understand that remark. I don't know what you are driving at.'

'Then I'll explain. Sweet and reasonable, that's me. Let's start at the beginning. Chambers approached you to try to fix the development scheme – get it a smooth passage through committee and council. You agreed, for an appropriate cut. You held on to Crampton House in the meanwhile, to avoid suspicion. You did the fixing, and got a sizeable bunch of the committee with you – the ones you could buy, and the few to whom subcontracting could be given. But you couldn't get enough to swing the committee, and you couldn't because the chairman was against you, and he had money and he had influence. You got balked, for three years, and you played clever, kept your real interest quiet, worked like hell behind the scenes – but you couldn't budge the chairman. Time dragged on, and you sweated, and your friends sweated – and still the chairman balked you.'

'Go on,' muttered Lorey with a sour twist to his mouth.

'Oh, I will, for I've got the picture, Lorey. Inevitably, with the passage of time, Chambers lost his financial backing and things got desperate. You needed two things: a hefty injection of capital and a swift passage through committee. Help in the first direction came with the arrival of our financial wizard – Joe Acton. He'd already shown his business acumen by spending seven years in jail after salting away a tidy little sum. He guaranteed that he'd find the capital for you – if he was cut in. So the group lined up – Chambers, the developer; Acton, providing the capital; you providing the front and the push in committee and council. Finance? Who else but Karel Martin, on the security of bonds ostensibly held by you but in fact provided by Acton? Martin fell hook line and sinker. But there was still one problem.'

'And that was?'

'The planning committee. You still couldn't budge Harry Kirk.'

'So?'

'So you killed him.'

Lorey started violently.

'You're mad! Crazy! Kill Harry Kirk?'

'What else could you do? You couldn't budge him; he was immovable. And what's more, you hated his guts. Not only was he standing in your way, preventing you from making a fortune, but he was the man who had been sleeping with your wife, and as far as I know, still was.'

Lorey was gasping with rage, his mouth opening and shutting like a stranded fish.

'You're … you… I'll break you for this, Iles … if you… I'll damn well…'

He was almost incoherent, and then suddenly the iron in the man showed, for he pulled himself together with an effort. He glared furiously at Iles, and a vein pumped in his forehead but when he spoke his voice was stiff, but controlled.

'You're talking nonsense, Iles.'

Iles grinned, and shook his head.

'You had the motive, my friend, and you know, it's a funny thing, I've not been able to discover where you were that night.'

'I don't have to account for my movements.'

'Not to me. What about the police?'

Lorey was quiet for a moment, staring fixedly at Iles. Then he said, 'I don't have to account for my movements – but I can, if it is necessary. You'll never prove that I was near Kirkley Hall. You'll never prove that I killed Harry Kirk. The way things are going it's his son who will be held guilty anyway. All I'll say is this – that bloody Harry Kirk needed killing, but you can't fix it on me. And don't try, do you hear me? Don't try!'

At the door he paused, with a sneer.

'As for the rest … there's not a damn thing you can do, Iles. By the time you got any proof that would stand up in court the deals would be through. So stick that, Iles!'

The door slammed loudly behind him.

Iles shambled across to the window and helped Centre climb in. He grinned a little sheepishly.

'Tough nut. I thought he might break, but he's not candyfloss.'

Centre walked across the room, and at Iles's nod switched on the gas fire, then stood with his back to it, warming the chills from his spine. He looked curiously at Paul Iles as the enquiry agent dropped into an easy-chair.

'How much of that,' he asked, 'can you actually prove?'

Iles lifted one shoulder in a doubtful gesture.

'Actually *prove* – not a great deal. But it's true enough – you saw Lorey's face! He's tied up with Chambers and Acton all right, just as I said.'

'What about the forged bonds?'

Iles enjoyed the question and his pleasure was reflected in his features.

'Well, that was just a bit of spice, really. I know there are bonds, but they're probably all right. I threw that one in just to cause a bit of consternation – it might even lead to some telephone wires humming tonight. Of course, I wouldn't put it past Acton to do it, but they'll think the same too, Chambers and Lorey, so there's no reason why I shouldn't help them towards an ulcer, is there?'

'And you think that Lorey did kill Harry Kirk?'

Iles's grin faded and he frowned.

'I think there's a strong chance that he did – but I can't find out where he was that night. On the other hand, he sounded pretty firm when he said he could account for his movements, if it was necessary.'

'Even if he couldn't, I still think it's not likely that–'

Iles lifted one hand imperiously. He squinted up to Centre and wrinkled his broken nose.

'Let's just look at the situation. Harry Kirk

is dead. It's called murder. Your client is charged. If he is not guilty, who is? Who else had the motive? For my money, James Lorey is out in front.'

'The way you say that, you imply that he is only one of several.'

Iles raised a ham fist.

'Let's just look at the list, my friend.'

He flicked up a finger.

'James Lorey himself. Not only has Kirk been blocking him off from a lot of money over a period of three years, but he was running around with Lorey's wife, and taking little trouble to hide the fact. Motive for murder?'

He flicked up a second finger.

'Joseph Acton. He has been under similar pressures to Lorey – he also wanted the Sandhill deal through – particularly if there does happen to be anything shady about the finance. And he also has another needle digging into him: he can hardly be enamoured of Harry Kirk, the man who prosecuted him. And remember, if that charge hadn't been made Acton might have been able to keep Western Utilities going, if not indefinitely at least for a considerable time. Money, and revenge. Motives for murder?'

He extended his third finger.

'Then there's Don Chambers.'

'He would never kill Harry Kirk simply because the man was holding up the scheme.

The motive is hardly strong enough.'

Iles looked at him wide-eyed.

'You would regard a million and a half quid as not presenting a motive for murder?'

Centre grimaced and accepted the point.

'You've named those three – I think we can add Lawson to the list too. I'm still not satisfied about his presence out at Kirkley Hall that night. I still think he was prowling, hoping to get his own back. Perhaps he did.'

'You pays your money,' agreed Iles, 'and you takes your choice of James Lorey, Joe Acton, Don Chambers and William John Lawson. My money is still on Lorey, or one of the first three…'

He paused thoughtfully.

'Or *all* of the first three.'

'You mean a conspiracy?'

'Well,' said Iles with a shrug. 'I've not been able to discover where Lorey was, or Chambers, that night. I wonder where Acton was? And couldn't they all have got together on the thing? Why one, as opposed to them all?'

Iles stood up and thrust his hands in his pockets, to walk irresolutely across to the window.

'Of course, all this discussion of motive, opportunity and action presupposes one thing.'

Centre knew just what he meant. It presupposed that Stephen Kirk had not murdered his father.

3

The course of the trial next day hardly made the supposition likely. Stanley produced the affidavits and written evidence of the police and Centre twiddled a pencil between his fingers as he listened. He was aware of Stephen Kirk beside him staring at Stanley like a fascinated rabbit in front of an aggressor. Stanley's tones as he read were clipped and precise.

'The first statement I wish to read is the evidence of Constable John Willis. It runs as follows.'

He began reading and Charles Miles leaned forward while his fellow justices displayed equal interest.

'…I had accompanied Sergeants Scott and Marton to Kirkley Hall in pursuance of further enquiries they were making into the deaths by arson of Mr and Mrs Harry Kirk. I remained outside on duty. From the front entrance it is possible to see the window of the garage and on seeing a flash of light in the window I proceeded to investigate. I shone my torch at the door and perceived that it was unlocked. As I entered the garage a door slammed at the back of the building and I realised that someone had left by that entrance. I passed through the garage and heard someone running in the paddock but saw no one. I called Sergeants Scott and Marton and together we searched the garage. We discovered what the intruder appeared to have been looking for.'

Stanley paused and flickered a quick glance in Stephen's direction. He moistened his thin lips, and continued:

'It lay under a pile of sacking, a one-gallon can used to hold paraffin. It was approximately half-full.'

Stanley flicked over the page.

'The can was taken away for examination.'

Centre glanced at Stephen; the young man's face was uncomprehending.

'What's all this about?' he whispered, but Centre was devoting his attention to Stanley.

'The second piece of written evidence that I wish to present is the affidavit of Dr Brian Adams of the Southampton Laboratory Service. Dr Adams is an analytical chemist of some repute. His statement reads as follows.'

Once again Stanley's mellifluous tones rolled around the courtroom.

'...the flask which I was given for examination–'

Stanley stopped, and looked to the Bench.

'I should explain here that a flask containing a small amount of paraffin, but wiped clean of any marks, was found in the bushes near the house. This will be substantiated by affidavit.'

He continued reading.

'...contained no marks and would seem to have been wiped clean. The can I was given contained almost half a gallon of paraffin. The neck of the can had been handled but marks were badly smudged. The body of the can did however contain various marks, including three clear imprints which were compared with fingerprints provided from police slides. There can be no doubt but that these two separate sets of prints are identical, and are the fingerprints of the same person.'

'What is he getting at?' whispered Stephen hoarsely. Centre waved him to silence. To the intent magistrates, Stanley was saying,

'This statement is supported by more detailed and technically worded depositions which will also be put into evidence.'

Centre was still. There was nothing yet on which he could take issue. No connection had yet been established between flask, can and the death of Harry Kirk. But Centre had no doubt that it would be coming.

Stanley was reading a police laboratory report. It stated that a small piece of rag submitted as having been found in the bedroom where the fire had taken place had been soaked in a small amount of paraffin.

Stanley smiled thinly.

'It is the police contention that the murderer took to the bedroom a small flask containing paraffin, which he had obtained from a can in the garage. It has been impossible to discover where the flask was bought. We cannot trace its ownership. But I refer again to Dr Adams's affidavit. He states that the flask was wiped clean. The contention of the prosecution is that the flask was thrown aside, as constituting no danger to the accused – but he had forgotten the can, which he had handled with bare hands.'

Stanley glared at the magistrates.

'The relevant papers and slides are tendered in evidence. Those fingerprints taken from the can are identical to those taken from the fingers and thumb of the left hand of the accused, Stephen Kirk.'

There were two further affidavits presented in evidence: one from the laboratory stating that the threads found on the iron-studded door at Kirkley Hall matched threads from a torn jacket worn by Stephen Kirk on the night of the murders. The second was made by a Linchester chemist, testifying to the regular supply of sleeping pills to Harry Kirk.

Stanley drew the whole thing together in his closing speech. He told how Stephen Kirk, unemployed, had come to Linchester, stayed at the Fortune Hotel, gone out to Kirkley Hall. In the garage he had poured paraffin from the can into a small flask; with this in his pocket and some rags in his hand he had entered the house where his father lay asleep under the influence of sleeping pills. Stephen had started a fire in the bedclothes with the paraffin and rags, staging an accidental death. He had waited only long enough for the fire to start before he left, wiping clean the flask and throwing it aside, carelessly. Perhaps he had intended going back to the garage also, for the can, but the screaming of Magda Kirk had started, lights had gone on, and he had panicked, and run. It was only much later, when police investigation had stated, that he had remembered the can bearing his fingerprints, and had tried to recover it, only to be disturbed by the police constable. But on the night of the murder itself he had overlooked it in his panic, had run down the drive to the main road, where he was seen but not immediately recognized by Lawson. Stanley referred again to the evidence of the hotel proprietor and the commercial traveller. The most despicable of crimes, Stanley sneered. The murder of one's parents, for the sake of gain and petty revenge.

All tied up in a neat bundle, thought Centre. What would another solicitor, a criminal practitioner, a more experienced advocate have made of it? Could he have torn into this evidence, shredded it, sought out its weaknesses? Would he have manipulated a strong defence?

But what was the defence?

Stephen could not remember. He admitted going to Kirkley Hall that night – if he had, why had he taken a can and a flask with him? Stanley had suggested that the flask was easier to carry in the house, and that Stephen had only thought of the can again after rumours of fresh police interest, sparked off by Lawson's visit to the police.

Centre shook his head. He was disturbed: there was the niggling thought in his mind that the cards were stacked *too* carefully, *too* neatly against Stephen. Life wasn't like that – it was untidy, irrelevant, unmotivated in a sensible way. The thought worried Centre.

The clerk of the court was speaking.

'...you will have an opportunity to give evidence on oath and to call witnesses. I am going to ask you if you wish to say anything in answer to this charge; you need not say anything unless you wish to do so; and you have nothing to hope from any promise, and nothing to fear from any threat, that may have been held out to induce you to make any admission or confession of guilt. Anything you say may be taken down and given in evidence at your trial. Do you wish to say anything in answer to the charge? You may make an unsworn statement from the dock; or you can give evidence on oath and call witnesses.'

It was obvious, of course: Stephen must

plead not guilty and reserve his defence. It was necessary. It was expected. It was done.

And as Miles and Acland and Edwards committed Stephen Kirk for trial at the next Assizes Centre could see in their demeanour that they believed Stephen Kirk to be guilty. They, and Stanley, and everyone else in the room. Even the people in the public seats, they were all convinced, and ... it had to be said, even David Centre was almost of that belief.

Until his eyes swept the room, the groups of faces, and suddenly, surprisingly, rested on one face. The face of a man he had met, just once, one evening.

The face of Brian Nathan.

CHAPTER VI

During the next three days the office seemed to exist in a vacuum; the aftermath of the preliminary hearing induced a void within which nothing seemed of much importance. Centre himself was unable to settle to any work, and he felt edgy in a way he could not understand. It was not only due to his mishandling of Stephen's defence in court, it was not only that he had failed to exercise any control over the prosecution's presentation of evidence, there was something else. It was the fact that something was eluding him, and he knew it, but could not put his finger on it.

When he had looked at Brian Nathan sitting there in court something had stirred in his mind, flickering out again before he could delineate it. He had called Paul Iles as soon as he had reached the office and Iles had said he'd poke some sticks under Brian Nathan's stones but the enquiry agent had been gloomy, and his attitudes were far divorced from his usual breeziness.

'I think we've run up against a brick wall,' he had grumbled. 'Those three – Lorey, Acton and Chambers – they're closer than ticks on a sheep. I've done all the checking I can and there's no chance that they were near Kirkley Hall that night.'

'Then where were they?'

'Lorey was at Number twenty-three, Grainger Road.'

'Don Chambers's house. And Acton?'

'My bet is that he was there too, but I wouldn't be able to prove it. It's why Lorey wouldn't tell us where he was, of course – the three of them would have been together discussing the Sandhill finagle. Lorey wouldn't want it known that he was involved – but he'd come clean like a shot if there was a threat of a murder investigation at his door.'

'They were probably discussing their financial backing. Who was it you said was backing them?'

'Karel Martin. Big or little, he'll back it provided there's money to be made at the end. Acton may be pulling the wool over his eyes but that's not our business. And Martin has been in the States for the last three months and is still there.'

'Martin … rings a bell, somehow. Anyway, what about Lawson?'

'I think you're barking up the wrong tree. It's true Lawson made a nuisance of himself and even got himself thrown off the estate but there's no evidence that he paid more than one visit there. And on the night of the murders, he was certainly drinking in the Green Man until 11.15 – at least, that's what his cronies will say, and that's what matters.'

'You said 11.15?'

'They have an arrangement with the landlord,' Iles had remarked caustically. He had hunched in his chair and squinted at Centre with a disconsolate expression. 'If you want my opinion,' he had added, 'I think you've reached the point of no return. You're throwing good money away, employing me further.'

Centre knew what he meant. The evidence against Stephen was circumstantial, but damning. It placed him at the scene of the crime and linked him with an implement used in the murder. And yet there was something … something that these three empty days had failed to produce. Centre sat at his desk and worried at the problem. Janet knocked on his door, and he called to her to enter.

'Mr Iles is here, Mr Centre.'

A few moments later Iles was dropping his bulk in the chair facing Centre. He looked in no happier frame of mind than when Centre had seen him immediately after the preliminary hearing.

'Brian Nathan?' prompted Centre.

Iles sighed.

'I checked, as you asked. Interesting, but

not very conclusive.'

'I told you that Nathan was at the coroner's and at the hearing last–'

'You did. I'm not surprised really – like many others he had little reason to be fond of Harry Kirk.'

'He had a motive for killing him?'

Iles pulled a face.

'Depends how you look at it – or how he did. You see, when Acton floated the Western Utilities company he wanted capital.'

'We come back to Acton again.'

'We do. Acton fooled Nathan. Convinced him that the company was a sound proposition and the bank, on Nathan's recommendation, advanced capital to the company. Nathan also told Harry Kirk that it was a good investment.'

Iles stretched his legs with a sigh.

'My feet...' he groaned. 'Anyway, Harry Kirk didn't put all that much in but it would seem that wasn't the point. He caught Acton over the books in his own firm, and then the Western Utilities frauds came to light. Kirk went spare. Money was money – however little. He screamed blue murder. He'd have sued Nathan and the bank for negligent misstatement–'

'But for the rule, well established in law, that there can be no liability for financial loss resulting from a negligent misstatement, providing the maker disclaims responsibility in the first instance.'

'Which,' agreed Iles, 'Nathan, like a good bank manager, had done. Anyway, Kirk still screamed – and someone heard him.'

'Who?'

'Head office. They didn't get rid of Nathan, of course. But they did the next best thing.'

Iles paused for effect.

'They buried him.'

'How do you mean?'

'They buried him, here in Linchester, even sent him to a smaller branch. They knew, he knows and I suppose Harry Kirk knew too that Nathan would never move again, never get promotion, and would rot there until he retired. Professionally, Harry Kirk cut Nathan's throat. True, he brought it on himself, but that's not the way Nathan would see it.'

'But it would hardly be a motive for murder,' Centre said in some doubt. 'And after so long...'

'Who can tell what's important to a man? And who knows what the trigger might be? Anyway, them's the facts, man. And there's nothing there, or connected with Nathan, that I can see is of much help.'

But there is, thought Centre, and it should be apparent to me. He was convinced there was something about Nathan, something that hovered in his mind like a butterfly, hesitant, unwilling to alight, evasive and continually just beyond reach.

But there all the same.

'All right, Paul,' he said, 'thank you anyway, you've done a good job–'

'Bit short on results, I'm afraid. Anyway, I'll keep sniffing – not on the payroll, I mean. If anything interesting does turn up, I'll be in touch.'

After he had gone Centre lounged moodily in his chair. There was a pile of paper work to be done but he could not buckle down to it for the dissatisfaction that rankled in his mind. He thought of Stephen, the cup of success in the Karnowski action dashed from his lips at the last moment. Centre rose abruptly and wandered miserably through to Janet's office. She looked up and smiled: the smile was tinged with anxiety. Probably worried about Stephen.

'Would you like some coffee, Mr Centre? I can make some, in a second.'

He nodded.

'You going to see Stephen tonight?' he asked.

'I don't think so. I gather they'll be moving him at the weekend … to Winchester. I … do *you* think he killed them, Mr Centre?'

It was a question he did not want to answer; it was one he refused to ask himself. He shrugged.

'I just don't know, Janet. If only he could remember – how he got that bruise on his face, how he tore his jacket on the brass studs on the door, what he did with that letter from his father–'

If there was a letter. Even now, Centre could not tell whether Stephen yet lied. The thought must have been reflected in his eyes, for Janet stood up briskly.

'I'll get the coffee.'

Centre sat on the edge of her desk, swinging one leg, staring at the floor. Hell! What *was* it about Nathan! There was *something*. He knew it. Nathan and Lorey, and Acton and Chambers.

It was gone again, a dancing butterfly. He cursed.

But someone cursed more loudly. The door leading to Blake's office swung open and Blake lurched in. He looked angry – but when he saw Centre sitting there his anger turned to consternation.

'Oh, I'm sorry, Mr Centre! I didn't see you – I mean I didn't realize that you were–'

'What's the matter, Charles?'

'Oh, it's nothing to bother you with,' said Blake, blushing slightly.

'Tell me.'

'No. I–'

Blake had something in his left hand, half hidden behind his back. Centre stretched out a hand and took it from him. *Parry: Law of Succession.* Centre smiled.

'Not busy, Charles?'

Blake shuffled uneasily, his face red. He looked like a rotund schoolboy caught kissing the headmaster's daughter.

'Well, I'd finished the Eltham conveyances and–'

'And you thought you'd do a bit of reading for the exams. There's nothing wrong with that, Charles. I don't mind – the work's done, so why not get down to the books? It's the firm benefits, in the long run.'

He flicked over the pages with his finger.

'But why the blasphemy?'

'I'm sorry, Mr Centre. It's just that my Latin was never very good and I got stuck on this thing and I just couldn't see what's what!'

'What is what?'

'The *commorientes* rule, Mr Centre.'

'You can't make it out?'

'Well, I can, basically, but it's the switch where it's an intestacy as opposed to a testate succession that confuses me.'

Centre grinned.

'Well, it's part of my duty as your principal to help sort it out. Now then, let's see … ah, yes, here we are. Right … now I'll take you through it, step by step, all right?'

Blake nodded.

'The word itself,' explained Centre, 'means dying together. It used to be a difficult problem where people died in a common disaster, you see, and had made wills leaving their property to each other, first, and then to others thereafter. If A dies first it all goes to B; if B dies first it all goes to A. It can apply to married couples too: and if there are no children it's important to Mr A's and Mrs A's relatives. Depending upon which died first, it could go to one branch of the family or the other, under the relevant will.'

Centre took a deep breath.

'Anyway, the problem is, if the two people died together in a common disaster it may be impossible to discover which died first. If they were both drowned at sea, for instance. To get around this problem, the *commorientes* rule states that in such an event, *the younger is deemed to survive the elder.* Thus, if A is the older, he is regarded as having died first, his property passes to B and thence under B's will.'

Blake nodded.

'I get that. It's a sort of rule of thumb. A legal way out of a difficulty. But it's the intestacy bit that throws me.'

Centre shrugged, and riffled through the pages of the textbook.

'It's quite simple really. The rule applies only if the two people die in circumstances where it is impossible to say which died first, and they have both made wills. If they die in such circumstances *without* having made wills, the *commorientes* rule simply has no application.'

Blake nodded again, but reluctantly.

'Yes … I get it, the rules of intestacy then apply. But, well, what would be the *practical* effect of the situation? I get the theory, but what would actually happen in such a case?'

The practical effect? Centre frowned. Well, it was quite straightforward. It would mean that…

It would mean…

His leg stopped swinging. He stood up and walked out of the room, ignoring Janet as she entered and leaving a surprised young legal executive behind him.

Brian Nathan.

And Acton.

And Karnowski.

When Janet followed him into his office she found him at his desk, staring out of the window. His mind was whirling with memories and questions. He neither saw Janet, nor heard her when she spoke.

'David – are you all right?'

When her face finally swam into focus he was aware of the curious anxiety in her brown eyes but it meant nothing to him, because his mind was full of tumbling questions and answers.

'You … you didn't answer when I spoke to you,' she was saying. 'I've brought your coffee.'

'Thanks,' he said mechanically, hardly aware of what she said for the pieces were clicking into place, not completely, for the outlines were still blurred, but clicking into place nevertheless; and the butterfly was in his net. And he could see the logicality of it all, the cold, horrible logicality of it and he was fascinated, unable to dismiss it from his mind.

Janet was leaving the room. He called to her, stopping her.

'Janet! A moment. I want you to do three things for me. I want you to contact Mr Iles at once. I want you to trace, and get me a telephone line to, a man in the States – a Mr Karel Martin. And … and I want you to bring me from the files the marriage certificate copy that was sent from Neuberg – concerning the marriage of Haren Karnowski and Magda Schneider.'

2

Janet was in reception when Centre walked into the office on Friday afternoon. She was talking to Marjorie but she broke off when he entered and at his nod led the way into her room.

'Mr Karnowski and Mr Kirk arrived about five minutes ago,' she said. 'I showed them straight into your room.'

'Did they arrive together?'

'No, but just a few minutes apart. Mr Kirk

– it's some time since I've seen him but he looks very much like Harry Kirk did. Though he looks ill, somehow – his face is a bit drawn, you know? I suppose Stephen's being committed for trial was a shock to him.'

'I suppose so. Now then, Janet, have you got the papers I asked you for?'

'Here they are, Mr Centre. Here is the transcript of your telephone conversation with Mr Martin. And here is the list of creditors of Western Utilities – Mr Iles brought it in this morning while you were at the bank with Mr Nathan.'

'Fine.'

Centre riffled through the papers. It was all there, all he needed, and enough to illustrate just how the pieces clicked into place.

'All right, I'll take these with me now.'

He entered his own room. John Kirk rose as he came in; Vasil Karnowski did not bother. Centre shook hands with both of them: Kirk, as Janet had said, was not looking well and there were fine lines etched around his eyes while his cheeks seemed more hollow than Centre remembered. Karnowski's bald head gleamed and the slow malevolence still burned in the man's cold eyes. Centre turned to John Kirk.

'And how are things with you, Mr Kirk?'

John Kirk essayed a tired smile. His eyes, under the flaring eyebrows, were pouched.

'Well enough,' he remarked, smoothing his expensive tie with a slim hand. 'Business remains brisk, but that's the case with all lawyers these days.'

Centre caught the sharp look that Karnowski shot in his brother's direction. It was as though the man suspected that Kirk's remark had been directed at him, a biting, a sniping. Centre remembered that Kirk had told him that he had advised Vasil Karnowski not to proceed with the action against Stephen on the illegitimacy issue – perhaps Karnowski now felt that, having lost the action, he was being criticized for ever bringing it and dragging the family name into court.

Though it was now in court anyway, and the criminal court at that. Centre dropped into the chair behind his desk and placed the papers he carried on the desk in front of him. He looked up to the two men facing him.

'I must first of all thank you for coming this afternoon, gentlemen,' he began, 'but the fact is that I would appreciate your advice. I am in a dilemma. I have been instructed to defend Stephen Kirk in this prosecution and I am ... ah ... somewhat worried as to what may be the best defence that we can raise. I thought it prudent and wise to ask you – as his nearest relatives – to attend for a conference on the matter.'

'I don't see what we can do,' grumbled Karnowski in a surly tone.

'Let's wait and see what is bothering Mr Centre.' John Kirk's voice was stiff with disapproval as he glared at his brother. Karnowski merely shrugged his shoulders, in a careless gesture.

'Well,' continued Centre, 'we shall obviously continue to plead not guilty, but you will be as aware as I am that the prosecution case against Stephen is a pretty strong one. I am also in some difficulty in framing an answer to the charge – for Stephen says he cannot remember.'

Kirk made a quick movement, which Centre interpreted as one of annoyance. Karnowski remained imperturbable. Centre watched the man for a moment, then went on,

'You may neither of you be aware of the fact that Stephen, some eighteen months ago, underwent an operation after an accident on a motorcycle. Scar tissue remains: the result is that when Stephen is under some stress he does, on occasions, drift into a semi-conscious state. It's almost a form of amnesia – and it would seem that this is why he cannot remember what happened at Kirkley Hall.'

'You mean he remembers *nothing?*' asked Kirk incredulously.

'Very little. The problem is, it's not a sound

proposition to put before a jury. You'll remember the Podola Case, Mr Kirk, and how that turned out.'

'Yes,' nodded Kirk, 'hysterical amnesia.'

Karnowski looked a little bewildered and then shrugged; he smoothed a hand over his bald head, patently bored.

'Perhaps we can get to the point,' he suggested in a guttural voice.

'I simply wanted to ask,' said Centre quietly, 'whether you might be able to help – agree upon some form of defence that would be of advantage to Stephen.'

'Hell!' Karnowski exclaimed. 'You two – you are the lawyers! Why bother me with it? If Stephen has head trouble why is it that you do not plead insanity and have done with it?'

Centre stared at Karnowski steadily. The cold eyes flickered away, and Centre continued.

'I don't think that a plea of insanity would meet with much success. But … there is the question of automatism.'

'There is what?' queried Karnowski.

'Automatism. It comes under the defence established by section 2 of the Homicide Act of 1957. I've got it here– I'll read it to you.'

Centre drew forward the Queen's Printer's copy of the Act and read out the marked passage.

'Where a person kills or is party to the killing of another, he shall not be convicted of murder if he was suffering from such abnormality of mind (whether arising from a condition of arrested or retarded development of mind or any inherent causes or induced by disease or injury) as substantially impaired his mental responsibility for his acts and omissions in doing or being a party to the killing...'

He closed the paper.

'I think that under this defence we can claim that Stephen was suffering a mental abnormality, temporary in nature, which made him unable to appreciate the quality of his acts – and indeed, now makes him unable to remember even what he did at all that evening at Kirkley Hall. I think that we can argue that he was in a state of unconscious automatism. There's a case, for example, a few years ago, of a man who slept with a woman he had casually picked up and who found her strangled beside him next morning. He was found not guilty of her murder: he had done it in his sleep. Unconsciously. Automatism.'

Karnowski frowned, then shook his head.

'As far as I am concerned, all this it is merely legal tricks and quibbling. For me, you can do just what it is you want with Stephen Kirk's defence. All of it is a matter of complete indifference to me. I am not concerned with this.'

Centre intercepted the look of pure dislike that flashed from John Kirk to Karnowski.

'So you are prepared,' said Centre, 'to agree that I should instruct counsel to use the defence of diminished responsibility?'

Karnowski shrugged expressively, and made no reply. John Kirk frowned.

'I'm not happy about it, Centre.'

'Why not?'

'I'm not happy about it,' Kirk said slowly, 'because it implies one thing. Indeed, it admits, not implies – if you put forward the defence of automatism you are as good as admitting that Stephen murdered Harry and Magda. You are saying that he is guilty. It is a dangerous plea. What if the jury think that he is lying over the fact that he cannot remember? He will as good as have admitted the commission of the crime – and he'll then be found guilty. I think you are wrong, Centre. I think you must plead not guilty, and move heaven and earth to discover what really happened. Try to get Stephen to remember, try to make him pull himself together. But diminished responsibility, no!'

It was curious the way emotion affected John Kirk – it changed the tone of his voice, and its inflections too. The veneer of his English accent peeled away and, though his English was still good, his accent betrayed his origins.

Centre turned to Karnowski.

'Is that your view also?'

Karnowski's eyes gleamed maliciously.

'I have no view about the matter. You will do as you please. Indeed, let us be frank. I do not give one damn what defence is used. As far as I know, and believe, Stephen killed his mother and father. He has no defence to the charge. The only pity about it all is that they do not hang convicted murderers these days! Because if they did I would get my rights. He would not get the money that my cousin left and it would come to me.'

Kirk rose, glowering in anger. Centre swivelled in his chair, observing the two brothers.

'You have a very strange view of our laws, Mr Karnowski – particularly for one who has used the law. You seem to know little about its effects, or how it works. Yet you rushed to court quickly enough when you thought you could get something out of it.'

Karnowski turned to snarl at Centre, but the solicitor was addressing John Kirk.

'Mr Kirk, are you at all familiar with the work of Robert Burton? In particular, with his *Anatomy of Melancholy?*'

'I cannot say that I am.'

'It was in that work,' continued Centre, 'that he made an interesting, and in our circumstances, an apposite remark. He wrote, and I now quote – *he who goes to law...*'

And Centre's glance flickered to the silent Karnowski.

'...*holds a wolf by the ears.*'

3

The door banged violently behind Vasil Karnowski.

'He seems upset.'

'He is an ignorant pig,' replied John Kirk with feeling.

'He was probably upset,' Centre said easily, 'because he did not understand what I was driving at with the quotation I gave. *You* understand it, don't you, Mr Kirk?'

John Kirk sat down again; he seemed tired and the lines around his eyes had become more marked.

'I don't follow you, Centre.'

'Perhaps you will in a moment, Mr Kirk. Suppose – that's a strange word, isn't it, *suppose?* So much of our lives depends upon supposition; our very actions are dictated by supposition. One thinks, suppose I do that – will he do the other? I wonder whether you would bear with me for a little while, Mr Kirk, while I indulge in a few suppositions?'

Kirk's head was back on the chair but his eyes were narrowed.

'Suppose away, my dear chap.'

Centre regarded John Kirk for a long moment and then nodded.

'All right, but I hope you'll not get bored while I ramble on. Let's suppose, in the first instance, that Stephen did not kill Harry Kirk. Let's suppose that he was killed by a man with money troubles.'

'You mean Vasil?' Kirk asked in some astonishment.

'The murderer needs money quite urgently. He discovers that Harry has asked Stephen to come to see him after all these years and he wants to prevent this happening – because it might lead to a reconciliation whereby Stephen will enjoy his father's estate after his death. The gentleman with the money troubles would be left out in the cold, financially. So, knowing that Stephen has an appointment for eleven a.m. next morning, and aware that Harry takes sleeping pills and retires about ten at night, the murderer enters the house and Harry's room. There lies Harry, asleep, perhaps breathing stertorously in his drugged state … the murderer splashes some paraffin, just a small amount, enough to start a fire quickly with some rags. He waits only to see the room ablaze and then he leaves Harry Kirk to die…'

Centre paused, and looked at his hands.

'Up to this point, the murderer's plan has gone smoothly. But then the first unexpected occurrence happens. As he leaves the house he sees someone near the house – perhaps he

can't get past unseen. So he attacks the man
– Stephen – who falls surprisingly easily, in
his half-drunken, semi-conscious state. And
as the murderer stares at Stephen he sees the
chance unexpectedly given him. He goes
through Stephen's pockets, removes Harry's
letter; he presses Stephen's hand against the
paraffin can; he drags Stephen to the door,
tears his coat on the studs. Now it can be
proved that Stephen was there – and the evidence that Harry had summoned Stephen is
gone.'

Centre stared at Kirk, silent in the chair.

'I don't think the murderer intended
Magda to die. But she was screaming when
Stephen came round. In a dazed and fright-
ened state he ran away, down the drive, into
the road, where he was seen by the prowling
Lawson.'

Kirk's features held a puzzled expression.

'I can hardly believe–'

'It is only supposition, of course,' Centre
said. 'But I think it is close enough to the
truth. The paraffin can, the coat, the disap-
pearing letter – these were just insurance. For
with Magda's death a problem had arisen –
I'll come back to that. The murderer knew
that murder was a dangerous business, he
knew there was a safer way to achieve his
objective. He hoped, in the first instance, that
the deaths would be regarded as accidental –
which they were, though the police remained

286

suspicious. He could hold the murder card close to his chest, then – and he could lead with the other trump in his hand.'

Kirk's eyes flickered up to his.

'The other trump?'

'The murderer was after Harry's money. Stephen stood in his way, but shakily, for there was some doubt about his legitimacy. So it was a matter of arranging a lawsuit to contest that legitimacy – the murder ploy could wait, lie fallow. Only when the lawsuit failed – as it did – would he need to play the next card. The murder card.'

'But how–?'

'The lawsuit wasn't going well. So he took a flask containing a little paraffin, wiped it clean of prints, and pushed it under the bushes, hoping it would be found. It was. It meant little, pointed to little, but it kept suspicions alive in police minds. Then he himself saw the police, hinted that he was worried about the circumstances surrounding the deaths. And he obtained help from an unexpected quarter: Lawson came forward at much the same time. The police made further enquiries, and while they were there the murderer went into the garage, placed the can, marked with Stephen's prints, in the garage and drew attention to himself with his flashlight. For he knew the time had come to play the second card – the lawsuit was failing. The police found the can, and the finger pointed to Stephen. Within days, the case against Stephen was sewn up, even tighter than the murderer could have hoped. Stephen couldn't remember, and his lies, so patent in quality, made his guilt more certain in everyone's mind. And if Stephen were found guilty of the murder of his father he could not succeed to the estate – the law says a man cannot profit from his crime. The real killer, in financial trouble, would win through once Stephen was convicted of murder. He would succeed to the estate – or half of it, at least.'

Kirk was shaking his head doubtfully.

'I don't see it. I would never have regarded Vasil as having the intelligence to plan such–'

'But *you* have the intelligence,' Centre said quietly. 'The intelligence, and the legal knowledge.'

The room was silent: Kirk's hand was frozen, gripping the arm of the chair. He glared at Centre, with the colour ebbing from his face.

'That joke was in bad taste.'

'No joke. You see, I wasn't sure until today. I guessed, but I wasn't sure. Now I am. I tested my suspicion – I asked you and your brother if you agreed with the automatism defence. Karnowski couldn't care less. *You* were against it.'

'My dear boy, I explained–'

'No. I know the real reason why you were against that defence. You knew the implications lying behind it. If Stephen were found guilty of murder he could not succeed to Harry's estate – you and Karnowski would share it. But if Stephen were not guilty by reason of insanity or diminished responsibility there was the possibility that he *could* take the estate – for it could be argued that he had not deliberately killed to gain the estate. Maybe the argument wouldn't have been a sound one, legally, but you didn't want to take that chance. So you were vehemently against my using that defence.'

Kirk brushed a hand over his eyes in a nervous, anxious gesture.

'Ingenious, and even entertaining, but as you said, merely supposition. I don't think–'

'Not all supposition. The fact is, I've been very slow. There have been a number of keys, which I've consistently ignored. They only began to click for me during the last couple of days – and they led me to the police, and to Brian Nathan, and to Karel Martin. It was then that I saw the sequence of events, and discerned the logic of it all – the legal logic, the lawyer's logic. *Your* logic.'

Kirk flicked a tongue across dry lips but made no reply.

'You had told me, when we met first, that you were rich,' continued Centre, 'and the local myth is that you are. After all, you are one of the Kirks. But at that first meeting of ours you were called to the telephone by a Mr Martin. It was only recently that I guessed it might have been Karel Martin. And when I spoke to him, over the transatlantic line, he eventually confirmed to me that you had borrowed money from him, a considerable amount. Then I asked myself, why did you need money?'

Centre paused; Kirk seemed a little breathless as he sagged in the chair.

'One of the keys clicked then,' continued Centre. 'Brian Nathan had been on my mind. I knew there was something and I remembered. At the Black Spider he told me that the Kirks were unlucky in things that mattered. For Nathan, a bank manager, things that mattered were *money*. He also said that local businessmen – the *unlucky* ones – lost a lot of money in the Western Utilities crash. That's why I checked with him, again today.'

Centre pushed across to Kirk the sheet of paper that Iles had left for him at the office.

'What Nathan told me is also confirmed by this list. It is a list of creditors of Western Utilities. You figure prominently among them.'

John Kirk made no move to take the paper. A nerve twitched in his cheek and his hand was shaking slightly.

'There were other keys,' Centre added. 'For instance, how could we regard Stephen's murdering as logical? He hadn't been in touch with his parents – he couldn't have known whether they had made wills or not. But *you* knew. The trouble was, I was preoccupied: I didn't see the Karnowski suit linked with the murders and I got bogged down looking for suspects in terms of a revenge motive. It wasn't until I broke away from Harry Kirk's enemies and looked away from a revenge motive that I saw light. And only then when I had occasion to think about the *commorientes* principle.'

Kirk still made no reply but his body sagged in the chair as he stared at Centre.

'Your relationship with Harry and Magda remained close over the years. You handled Magda's business affairs. Now when we first met you told me that Harry had left you a legacy and the bulk of his estate to Magda. In the event of Magda predeceasing him, you got the whole estate.

'Magda's will, on the other hand, named Stephen, left everything to him. Now, you loved Magda, you would never have dreamed of hurting her. But if you killed Harry, what would happen? His property would go to her, and you conducted her business affairs. That meant that you would have control of Harry's money while Magda lived, and you could keep Martin at bay. It must have been only after you left Southcliff and had time to think that you realized the problems that arose when Magda died accidentally in the same fire as Harry.'

Kirk made an involuntary gesture with his hand; Centre waited, expecting him to make a protest but when Kirk remained silent he continued.

'They died in the same fire. It would be impossible to say which died first. They had both made wills, so the *commorientes* principle applied. When I checked the Neuberg certificate, I saw that *Magda was younger than Harry.* That would mean that she would be deemed to have died after her husband; it meant that Harry's property would pass to her, and the estate would then pass under *her* will, not Harry's. *Everything would go to Stephen.*'

Centre stared without compassion at the man in the chair. John Kirk was shivering slightly, but it could not be that he was cold. He was reliving those days, those events, and he could not bring himself to stop Centre speaking.

'It says a great deal for the quickness of your wits that you planned it thereafter with such precision and efficiency. You realized that you could not afford to let the wills stand: not if you were to keep Martin at bay. Stephen was named as beneficiary, and therefore would take all. But then a thought struck you – if there were no wills, what would happen then? First, the *commorientes* rule would have no application, obviously. Second, the property would go to the next of kin. It would pass under the rules of intestacy. But the rules of intestacy state that property can go only to legitimate children. So Stephen would be entitled to everything – *but only if he were legitimate.*'

Kirk was shaking his head slightly, and his lips moved but no sound came forth. His eyes were riveted to Centre's face.

'On the night of the fire, almost instinctively, you had taken certain precautions when you found Stephen there. But it would be a dangerous card to play, the murder card. You couldn't be *sure* that Stephen would be regarded as a murderer – but you did have reason to believe that there might be a chance that Stephen could be shown to be illegitimate. That ploy could bring half the estate to you, if successful. And only if that ploy failed could you risk playing the murder card.'

Centre rose, and walked out from behind his desk to stand over Kirk.

'So you went ahead with the scheme. You suppressed both wills and said that they'd been lost in the fire. I thought it strange that no copies had been kept but I wasn't suspicious for it seemed to be contrary to your interest to suppress them: after all, you were a legatee under both. You suppressed the wills and let Karnowski know his rights – although you were careful to take Stephen's side to avoid suspicion. You knew that Karnowski's impecunious state and his cupidity would press him to action. You also tried to stack the cards by asking an inexperienced solicitor to take Stephen's case. You hoped that I would botch it – I was vain enough at the time to think you felt I could handle it. I now know you were hoping I couldn't. I guess also that it was you, not Karnowski, who engaged those thugs in Neuberg, to try to destroy the certificate. That failed, and the Karnowski case was slipping away. So you decided to play the murder card...'

Kirk's face was ashen.

'I was never near Kirkley Hall that night. I was–'

'At a hotel in Southcliff. You told me. Your car had broken down, and it probably had. Did you engineer that? I've got an enquiry agent in Southcliff right now. Will he find a car hire firm there? Will he find a booking to a man of your description? Will there be a logging in the relevant car of about one hundred and thirty miles for that night? What will the answers be, Mr Kirk?'

Kirk was shaking, visibly. He looked old, in a grey, careworn way and there was a defeated air about him that was uncharacteristic of the man. Centre felt almost sorry for him, and then he remembered Magda Kirk, the woman of whom all spoke well, and he hardened. Then it was as though the thought was transmitted for Kirk shuddered and spoke her name and as he did so his resolve seemed to crumple.

'Magda... I thought that she was away that night. If I had known... I thought that she'd gone, I never wanted her to die. I adored her ... she had been a mother and a sister to me, and more, she would have been more, I'm sure of it. But Harry, that pig Harry, he got her pregnant and then he watched her die inside here in Linchester. She was never happy here with him, not really happy. And but for him there could have been...'

He looked up but Centre felt that he saw nothing. The death of Magda Kirk had been eating away at the man, ravaging him, destroying him.

'It was why I left them, to set up in practice in Linthorpe. I couldn't stay in the same house and be so near to her – but neither could I go far away. And I watched her grow older and I saw him twisting her life out of shape. Then there was Stephen, turned away, that hurt her deeply, but she never railed against him...'

He shuddered.

'It was when Martin was pressing me for more money that Harry became suspicious and discovered that I ... I had been using Magda's trust funds to pay some of the terrible debts that I incurred when Western Utilities crashed seven years ago. And I took those shares on Harry's advice! Yet he refused to help me later, with all his thousands. For years I managed to keep up appearances but I needed money and when Harry discovered my defalcations over the trust fund he said he was going to tell Magda, ruin me, draw up a new will.'

He looked down at his hands; they were shaking.

'He was going to tell Magda. It was then that I decided to kill him.'

'And you blamed his son.'

Kirk looked up quickly but his eyes were still vacant, dreaming.

'*Stephen* ... he lay at the base of the whole thing but although he stood in my way, I had no real dislike of him, I didn't *want* to hurt him. After all ... he was Magda's son. But what could I do? What else could I do? Harry was going to destroy me, Martin was pressing me, ruin and disgrace and possibly even prison faced me – I had to kill Harry! And after that, I had to go on, I had to plan, I had to think, think, think ahead of the pack...'

An expression of mingled pain and distress flickered across John Kirk's face, and he buried his head in his hands.

'But her ... Magda ... I never intended ... not her. I ... I loved her.'

His voice died to a demoralized whisper.

'And without her, now, it all seems so pointless.'

4

Iles grimaced with a certain satisfaction as he faced Centre across the sunlit desk.

'So the wolf turned, finally, and savaged him. There's something that's almost biblical in the situation, don't you think?'

Centre nodded.

'Yes. But I should have seen earlier that it was John Kirk who was riding that wolf. I was too concerned asking you to chase up Acton and Lorey and Lawson and Chambers–'

There was a tap on the door and Janet backed in with the two cups of coffee that Centre had asked for. After she had left again Iles smiled.

'Nice girl. Wasn't there something at the back of my mind about her and Stephen–?'

'I wouldn't want to look at the back of your mind! But it may be that for once you are right, in this instance. However, I was looking at the *Linchester Gazette* this morning and I was somewhat surprised to see the front page splash.'

'Yes?'

'Yes. They've run a leader and headlines about a certain development scheme. They're screaming for a public enquiry – and what's more, they're naming names. To us, rather familiar names. I … er… I just wondered how come they got the information so … er … quickly, you know?'

'I have not the faintest idea,' Iles said innocently.

'I'm sure.'

'Anyway, will John Kirk have a defence to the charge of murder – I take it, incidentally, that *you* won't be defending him!'

'Well, he didn't ask me to, strangely enough. As for his defence, no, I can't see that he's got one. Straight premeditated murder. But to return to the subject you want to avoid – did you discover whether those securities of Lorey's were forged by Acton?'

Iles shrugged.

'It's probable that they were all right; even if they weren't, Karel Martin isn't going to squeal about them for he's got a financial reputation to lose, and I don't think he'll pull out of the Sandhill scheme anyway.'

'Provided it gets through this public enquiry demand.'

'There is many a slip,' Iles said, affecting a look of sagacity and rising to his feet. 'However, I must be away. Affairs of state, you know.' He extended a huge hand. 'It's been a pleasure doing business, Mr Centre.'

'We must do it again,' Centre said soberly.

After Paul Iles had gone Centre slumped down in his chair. He felt rather tired, but he had no doubt that a stiff whisky would sort that out. On the other hand, tiredness was one thing, a slight feeling of depression was another. Particularly when he could not suspect its cause. After a while he rose and wandered through into Janet's office. She was busy typing; she looked up when he entered but did not speak and he watched her at work for a moment. At last, casually enough, he said,

'I … er … I gather that Stephen Kirk called in this morning while I was out.'

'That's right.'

He waited but Janet made no attempt to expand upon her statement.

'Was he looking for me?'

'No.'

'Oh.' Centre hesitated, then blurted out. 'He came in to see you, then.'

'Right again.'

The hell with it, thought Centre.

'What did he want?'

Janet raised her eyebrows, looked squarely at Centre, and replied.

'He asked me to marry him.'

'What did you–?'

She cut in before he could finish.

'I turned him down.'

'Why on earth did you do that? I thought...'

His words died away. Janet muttered under her breath, then pulled out a rubber from her desk and began to attack the letter she was typing. Only when she had stopped rubbing the lacerated paper did she look up, with a slight flush to her cheek.

'Well,' she said, 'a girl has to take a chance once in a while. After all,' and when she looked at him there was no mistaking the expression in her eyes, 'a girl doesn't know what ... what else may turn up, does she?'

The publishers hope that this book has given you enjoyable reading. Large Print Books are especially designed to be as easy to see and hold as possible. If you wish a complete list of our books please ask at your local library or write directly to:

Dales Large Print Books
Magna House, Long Preston,
Skipton, North Yorkshire.
BD23 4ND